Dedalus Africa
General Editor: Timothy

Our Musseque

José Luandino Vieira

Our Musseque

Translated by Robin Patterson

Dedalus

This book has been selected to receive financial assistance from English PEN's translation programme. English PEN exists to promote literature and our understanding of it, to uphold writers' freedoms around the world, to campaign against the persecution and imprisonment of writers for stating their views, and to promote the friendly co-operation of writers and the exchange of ideas.

Published in the UK by Dedalus Limited,
24-26 St Judith's Lane, Sawtry, Cambs, PE28 5XE
email: info@dedalusbooks.com
www.dedalusbooks.com

ISBN printed book   978 1 910213 07 0
ISBN ebook   978 1 910213 21 6

Dedalus is distributed in the USA by SCB Distributors,
15608 South New Century Drive, Gardena, CA 90248
email: info@scbdistributors.com   web: www.scbdistributors.com

Dedalus is distributed in Australia by Peribo Pty Ltd.
58, Beaumont Road, Mount Kuring-gai, N.S.W. 2080
email: info@peribo.com.au

Publishing History
First published in Angola in 2003
First Dedalus edition in 2015

Nosso Musseque © copyright Luandino Vieira, Lisbon: Caminho 2003 published by arrangement with Literarische Agentur Mertin Inh, Nicole Witte.K. Frankfurt am Main, Germany.
Translation copyright © Robin Patterson 2015

Printed in Finland by Bookwell
Typeset by Marie Lane

For Linda

The Author

José Luandino Vieira was born in Portugal in 1935 and grew up in Luanda. He was one of a group of political activists whose trial in 1959 helped spark the Angolan uprising against colonial rule. He spent most of the following fifteen years in prison or under house arrest, until the collapse of the Portuguese dictatorship in 1974.

His first collection of short stories, *Luuanda*, written in prison, was awarded the Grand Prize for fiction by the Portuguese Writers' Society in 1965, resulting in the society's closure by the Salazar regime. Following Angolan independence, he held a number of important literary and cultural roles under the new Angolan government, including secretary-general of the Angolan Writers' Union. He has published two novels, *Nós, os do Makulusu* (1974) and *Nosso Musseque* (2003), two novellas and seven collections of short stories, along with two parts of his *De Rios Velhos e Guerrilheiros* trilogy. In 2006 he was awarded, but declined for personal reasons, the Camões Prize, the most prestigious international award for literature in the Portuguese language.

He now lives in Portugal.

The Translator

Robin Patterson came late to literary translating, after pursuing other careers in various parts of the world. He has participated in both the Birkbeck and the BCLT literary translation summer schools and was mentored by Margaret Jull Costa in 2013 as part of the BCLT mentorship programme.

His translated extracts from José Luís Peixoto's *Inside the Secret* were serialised in 2014 by Ninth Letter, and his translation of *Eve's Mango*, an extract from Vanessa da Mata's debut novel, was featured on the Bookanista website. He also contributed a translation of *Congressman Romário: Big Fish in the Aquarium* by Clara Becker to The Football Crónicas, a collection of football-related Latin American literature published by Ragpicker Press in June 2014.

Our Musseque by José Luandino Vieira is his first translation for Dedalus.

Contents

Zeca Bunéu and Others   13

The Truth about Zito   87

Carmindinha and Me   157

Translator's Note   187

Kilombelombe kejidiê ku dimuka: kama ka-mudimuna

– as Don'Ana used to say, when talking about
Carmindinha

Zeca Bunéu and Others

I

When someone has a nickname, there's usually a reason. I always stuck to that simple fact whenever luck brought Zeca Bunéu, Carmindinha and me together and we remembered Xoxombo. Tunica, too, was gone – life and her passion for rumbas and sambas had carried her away to Europe. A lost soul, said Mrs Domingas sadly. Life's a big thing and words can't change it, I said by way of an excuse. Carmindinha said nothing, keeping her opinions to herself, but we knew how much it hurt her to think about her sister.

Sometimes we met in Mrs Domingas's house, when I was going out with Carmindinha. Zeca Bunéu would stop by a bit later, calling for me with his usual whistle but always ending up by joining in the conversation. And before then, more times than I can remember, we'd sit with Mrs Domingas, already old and white haired, and Bento Abano, still silently reading the newspaper without glasses in his corner. We always talked about Xoxombo, even as the tears rolled down Mrs Domingas's wrinkled face. Carmindinha always told the same story about the boy's nickname, and she wouldn't hear of any other version. But Zeca Bunéu, always the mischievous *musseque* boy and with his particular knack for telling things just the way he saw them, told the other story, the one all the other kids knew. My opinion on the subject didn't count. It's true that I liked watching Zeca tell the story the only way he knew how – hands waving wildly, screeches of laughter and exaggerated winks from those big eyes of his. But it was with tender love that I watched Carmindinha – warm, kind, sometimes angry – as she stuck up for her brother. It was only when Mrs Domingas began to weep at all the memories we'd dredged up and Bento started coughing in his cane chair that I'd interrupt. Not very helpfully, I confess. I only said what everyone was saying: when someone has a nickname there's usually a reason for it, and if everyone called Xoxombo the same thing, then there's no point going on and on about where it came from.

Then the conversation would change. The sea, the islands and the winds came rushing in as Captain Bento began to speak. Mrs Domingas would go to the little cupboard and bring out some homemade liquor for everyone (corn beer for Zeca since that was the only thing he liked) and we all drank. Carmindinha sat sewing and I watched the captain and Zeca discussing the sea, only joining in when it came to talking about our newspaper or the ones the captain used to write for back in the old days. Then, beneath the little hum of conversation, Mama Domingas would start to nod off and that was the signal for us to leave.

Carmindinha would come with us to the door, let me touch her small, round breasts underneath her loose robe, and stand there watching the two of us disappear into the night. Whenever we had these conversations about Xoxombo, Zeca Bunéu and I would wander aimlessly around the sleeping city, talking about the boy and our old shanty town, our *musseque*.

Today, All Souls' Day, I met Carmindinha at the entrance

to the old cemetery. It was our first meeting since our big falling out all those years ago and this time there was no need to talk about Xoxombo – he was everywhere around us, in the black clothes and the lingering scent of lilies. From that moment on, his story just wouldn't leave me alone. Time had already consumed all the small, insignificant details and shone light on what really mattered. During all these years apart from Carmindinha, I'd shunned her gentle influence, her well-meaning kindness in standing up for her brother. And without Carmindinha there, Zeca Bunéu and I never again spoke of Xoxombo.

Perhaps now, with all the things that life and the passing years have taught me, all the different voices I've heard, perhaps now I can tell Xoxombo's story properly. If I don't succeed, it isn't his fault, nor because of all that nonsense about his nickname. The fault's mine, for putting literature where once there was life, for replacing human warmth with anecdote. But I'll tell the story anyway.

1

So when was it, then, that all the women came out, laughing and chatting from door to door, to celebrate the return of ship's master Captain Bento de Jesus Abano and his family, back among all their old friends in our *musseque*? According to Carmindinha it was all long before I arrived, before I came to live here with my stepmother. Later on, relations cooled with Zeca Bunéu's dad, the shoemaker, who lived next door. What with all his white friends, there were times when the two men spoke only when necessary, to apologise when the hens went scratching around where they shouldn't, or when their kid goat *Espanhola* snapped the rope tying her to the trunk of the big *mulemba* tree, munched through the fresh green cassava leaves, knocked over the water cans or even made holes in the fence.

Then there was all that fuss when Zeca Bunéu stole a few poems by Silva Xalado, one of the coloured guys who worked for his dad, and made fun of him in front of everyone. His father just laughed at Zeca's wise-cracking and it was then that Bento Abano's family began to distance themselves, saying it just wasn't right letting a youngster make fun of someone like that, poor guy, no mother or father – people deserved more respect than that. So the evenings sitting round the doorstep stopped and, little by little, the other women – even the wife of Mr Augusto, Biquinho's dad, who lived quite far away – started coming to Mrs Domingas with little neighbourly gifts, asking to borrow this and that, or volunteering their children to take *Espanhola* to graze on the new grass up beyond the baobab tree. Mrs Domingas, a good soul, was greatly moved by these gestures of friendship, and Bento also liked being back among 'his people', as he put it.

Carmindinha was growing up fast – she'd put away her toys, stopped playing with us younger ones and was always cleaning and tidying, mending clothes, and helping her mother in the kitchen. Mrs Domingas eagerly praised her daughter's quick hands and aptitude for housework.

'Ah sisters!' she told all her friends and neighbours, 'this one's more like it. As for that Tunica, well I can't even get her to go and fetch the water. Spends the whole time just drumming on the bottom of the water can and even the walk takes her half an hour. But when it comes to my older girl? Just you see – she'll go far, I'm telling you, sisters. It's just a pity that Bento won't hear of sending her to get proper lessons. Fingers nimble as a bird, sisters, nimble as a bird!'

As these discussions and controversies continued, the rains petered out and the cool season settled in, the grass dried out for the kids' bonfires and the sun took a breather. But it wasn't long before it was back, a little stronger each day, hotter and yellower and fiercer, and the winds began once again to blow heavy wet clouds in off the sea. Once again the downpours coursed through the sands of the *musseque*, green grass sprouted everywhere, cashew nuts ripened and life carried on as normal – boys playing games after school, mothers and daughters talking about their daily chores, about who'd done what, who'd said what and who'd been arguing with whom.

As time passed, the quarrels cleared like smoke from a fire. Mrs Domingas and Bento Abano started speaking to their white neighbours again – in poor neighbourhoods like ours it's a simple fact that people can't stay angry for long. And so for many months the *musseque* settled into an everyday calm, disturbed only from time to time by the noise of the kids' games, the odd squabble here and there and all the usual carry-on of life.

More and more people were taking notice of Carmindinha. First she sewed shorts for the kids, then little shirts and then, one afternoon, all the women from the neighbouring houses came over to congratulate her on a pretty cotton dress she'd made for Tunica.

'Oh, she's not a little girl any more!'

'That's what I've been telling you, sister. It's just a pity Bento can't…'

'I know, I know. But I've heard there's a school downtown that doesn't charge anything!'

'That's what they say, sister Sessá! Yes, that's what's they say! But I don't believe it. Free? For blacks and coloureds? Sorry, but I just don't believe it.'

'But it is, sister Domingas, really it is! It's run by the League. Matias, God rest his soul, his daughter told me – she goes there. She came round here yesterday afternoon with a message from her aunt, and that's when she told me.'

'Tssssk!' Mrs Domingas sucked her teeth scornfully. 'Oh, for goodness' sake! If it was coming from someone… But that Joanica, the one whose mother passed away? *Sukuama*! I don't believe it! There might be a school, but it's a school for sluts!'

Carmindinha, who'd been enjoying the praises of the older women, joined in. 'It's true, mama. Joanica's telling the truth. She's already told me. Mr Gaspar's daughter Teresa is going there as well. Honestly, mama, you don't need to pay.'

'All right, all right! If that's how it really is, then one of these days I'll go down to see my friends in Coqueiros and find out for myself.'

The neighbours solemnly nodded their agreement, still praising Carmindinha's handiwork as they left and promising little jobs for her to do. When they'd all gone, mother and daughter sat together on the big cane chair and carried on talking in low voices. Bento wasn't there, he'd gone out to fetch young Xoxombo from the Mission School and Tunica had wandered off to play with the other girls up beyond the baobab tree, leaving *Espanhola* to nibble at weeds growing out of the walls round the backs of the houses.

And so it was one of those hot, dark nights when all the fuss erupted.

Earlier that day, towards evening, Mrs Domingas, swathed in the beautiful cloth that Bento had brought her from Matadi and wearing her patent leather sandals, made her way with young Tunica down the sandy paths into the city, crossing Ingombota on their way to Coqueiros. Later on, well past midnight, we all began to hear noises – the scrape of furniture, loud voices, a few shrieks from Mrs Domingas, and Carmindinha, Tunica and Xoxombo bleating like goats at the door. There was no moon and the *musseque* was in complete darkness, just a few palm oil or paraffin lamps beginning to flicker from the houses. One by one, the women from the neighbouring houses came over, clutching their robes tightly round them and followed by the men, some still pulling on their trousers. They asked the children what was going on, but their only response was yet more sobbing. Mrs Domingas drew courage from the neighbours now standing round her front door, and you could hear the anger in her voice.

'It's God's own truth! Go ahead and beat me – I won't complain. Even kill me if you like and I won't complain! But that girl is going to school to learn to sew. Yes, she is – you mark my words!'

You could hear more sounds of furniture being pushed around and then Bento's loud voice drowning out all the tears and the sobbing.

'Over my dead body! I've said it once and I won't say it again. No daughter of mine is going downtown, and that's final. Coming back up here dressed up like a white woman, wearing lipstick and heels? Never, never, never for as long as there's a Captain Bento Abano in the house!'

Carmindinha stood in the doorway, her voice choked with angry tears. 'But I really want to, dad! There's no harm in it. I just want to learn to sew – how many times have I told you?'

She ran off, scared, and everyone else shrank back as Bento emerged from inside. In the dark all you could make out were his long, white undershorts. Taking advantage of the gathering crowd, Mrs Domingas shrieked: 'Help! Help me, neighbours! Bento's going to kill me! Just because I want my daughter to become a seamstress, because I want her to be a proper dressmaker rather than slaving over the washing and ironing every day!'

She was sobbing now. Bento carried on with his speech about the life of perdition down there in the city, immorality sneaking up on people and the setting of bad examples – all in a booming voice that no one would ever have thought the softly spoken captain capable of.

'I've said it once and I'll say it again: I'm the one who gives the orders! Any daughter of mine will be brought up the way her mother was, the way her grandmother was, the way her people were. I'm not going to let her become a lost soul down in the city. A sewing course? Huh! Well I know what that'll lead to. She'll no sooner be sewing than she'll be dropping her knickers in some dark alley and turning up back here with child in her belly. And as for who the father is, well that'll be anyone's guess. No, not my girl, never!'

What with all the noise and everyone's attention focused on the captain's house and the bawling kids, nobody saw Albertina's client slip away while she, huffing and puffing, came out of her hut, crossed over, unceremoniously pulled the kids out of her way and went into the captain's house.

Everyone just stood there, astonished. How on earth could Albertina have the brass neck to go into that hut when the whole *musseque* knew she barely exchanged so much as a good morning or good afternoon with Mrs Domingas, on account of some old quarrel almost everyone had long since forgotten?

But the white woman had already gone inside. 'For Christ's sake!' she barked in her wine-soaked voice. 'Let's have a bit of civilisation around here, shall we? Why don't you all just shut up and someone light a lamp!'

A hand passed her a lit match, and Albertina felt around

for a lamp to light. Caught in the yellow glow that suddenly filled the small room, Mrs Domingas was crouched in a corner in her underclothes, her large bosom heaving as she sobbed. Bento stood embarrassed in the darkest part of the room, his undershorts reaching down to his knees, his hands in front of his belly, trying to conceal his bony, hairy body. Albertina had appeared so quickly that the captain was left frozen, speechless. She immediately took charge of the situation.

'*Sukuama*! Can no one get along in this *musseque* any more? I work all night, I get no sleep all day, and still my own neighbours won't leave me in peace? As for you miserable lot outside, why don't you all just bugger off home rather than standing round here like donkeys with those silly grins on your faces? And you, mister-high-and-mighty ship's captain with your rusty old boat – get some clothes on, pronto! You should be setting an example to these kids. Is this what people mean by 'family life'? Bloody hell! Don't you know how to talk things over like decent people? Nothing but a bunch of savages! And hitting the poor, miserable woman like that – is that how a real man behaves?'

Some of the other neighbours had ventured inside and were helping Mrs Domingas to cover herself up and sit down on the chair. Tunica and Xoxombo ran over to their mother; Carmindinha went into the bedroom and came back with her father's trousers. Once he was dressed the old captain recovered some of his dignity and, speaking more softly now, went round apologising to everyone but saying that an argument between man and wife is for the man and wife to sort out. Then, skilfully as ever, with that calm voice and good manners for which he was famous throughout the *musseque*, he begged the neighbours not to spoil a good night's sleep – better to go back to their beds because there was nothing more to see here.

23

The women lingered a while, making sympathetic noises and lacing their farewells with many words of advice, until, finally, Mrs Domingas was left alone with Tunica and Carmindinha. Bento, ashamed, had gone back inside with Xoxombo and the neighbours heard him turn the lock. Albertina, wiggling her generous backside, smirked mischievously from her doorway.

'It's a pity you're so old, sister Domingas! I'd teach you a remedy for that rusty old sea captain of yours. Now just you keep him waiting a couple of days. Or send him over to me and I'll put some lead in his pencil!'

Mrs Domingas fixed her with a smile and, pulling her two daughters towards her, replied smugly, 'Well now, look who's talking! Don't you worry, Albertina, I've no need to spice things up. Anyway, I've got what I wanted – that girl of mine's going to sewing school!'

Silence slowly returned to the *musseque* night, snuffing out one by one the little groups of gossip and laughter until only the white woman, Albertina, remained sitting on her doorstep, brushing her hair and talking to her mongrel.

So no one was the slightest bit surprised the next morning when, as soon as Bento left the house to take Xoxombo to school at the Mission, Mrs Domingas set off downtown with Carmindinha, her hair neatly brushed and looking so smart in a dress she'd made herself, down the old path towards Ingombota and into the city.

The neighbours' broad smiles that afternoon, and their knowing glances at Bento as he sat on the doorstep reading his newspaper when Carmindinha, Teresa and Joanica returned with their papers in hand, were confirmation of Mrs Domingas's victory. When he caught sight of the girls, Captain Abano folded his newspaper and, saying he was off to fetch Xoxombo and *Espanhola*, headed up the track away from the city.

2

What with Carmindinha going off to her sewing and Xoxombo at school down at the Mission, Tunica was left feeling fed up and angry. She began to grumble about fetching the water day in day out when it was so far away. Mrs Domingas couldn't do it herself any more, and now on top of everything there was *Espanhola* to be taken grazing every evening, and the grass nearby had all been nibbled bare. And every time she went off to hang around with the other girls there'd always be the old captain warning her about something or other.

'Careful, Tunica! Don't let Mr Viriato's goat anywhere near *Espanhola*! Don't leave *Espanhola* on her own! Make sure you take good care of our little goat!'

Tunica always left the house tutting loudly and rolling her eyes – all she wanted to do was go down to the shop and listen to sambas and rumbas on the radio. But there was no school for Xoxombo on Saturdays, so that's when it was his turn to take the goat grazing. He really liked the job, sitting under the baobab tree, firing off pebbles with his slingshot and studying his geography and science. Zeca Bunéu and the others usually went up there with him, putting the long afternoons to good use by setting traps and bait for the birds, or wandering off through the sandy scrub to search for things in the piles of rubbish and wait for their friend to whistle when the birds came.

Captain Abano didn't need to give Xoxombo any special advice. He trusted his son and knew the boy was handy with the slingshot – he'd hit countless goats' horns with his pebbles. Sometimes he'd climb up the path to the open pastures just to watch over the boy while he was working. The two of them would stay up there, sitting under the tree and going over the boy's geography lessons – he was already a genius at it, asking questions even his father, the proud ship's master who'd sailed all the way up to the lush green isles of São Tomé and all the way down to Walvis Bay, couldn't answer.

Xoxombo always kept a close eye on Mr Viriato's goat – the big, ugly one with a dirty beard under his chin who was always chasing the nanny goats. Mrs Domingas was always telling him the old billy goat was dangerous and to keep his wits about him – *Espanhola* was still too young and she didn't want her mated.

That afternoon the main flock was grazing nearby. The cool season was approaching and the nanny goats were scattered here and there throughout the long grass, nibbling the last green shoots from the rains and calling to their little kid goats who ran and jumped around them, pretending to fight with each other. The other boys tending the goats all sat together under a big *muxixi* tree, occasionally whistling or firing off pebbles to bring the flock scrambling back together again before carrying on grazing, flicking away the flies with their ears. The old billy goat was on his own, further away, but a sea breeze blowing in from Mussulo Bay carried his scent down to the baobab tree where Xoxombo was sitting. The boy had tethered *Espanhola* close by, in the middle of a lush bit of grass, and he could hear her munching away, occasionally bleating back to her friends a little further away. From time to time Xoxombo put his book down and looked over towards Cinco, where Zeca and the others were playing among the twisted old cashew trees, or down towards the path, waiting for the captain to come and give him another geography lesson. And so with a fresh breeze pushing white clouds across the sky, the evening peacefully drawing in and *Espanhola* close by, Xoxombo immersed himself completely in the drawings in his book.

And that's where the stories diverge.

According to Zeca Bunéu and the other *musseque* boys who were up there, young Xoxombo decided to misbehave with little *Espanhola*. And that's why the big black billy goat charged him and gored the boy with his horn. Even today, nobody can understand why Zeca and the others always tell the story like that. It's true that Xoxombo had changed after all the Zito drama, but he wasn't a bad kid like they make out. Still, Zeca swears it happened exactly how he tells it, that he saw it with his own eyes and so nobody can argue with what he says. What's more, it was Zeca who reached the *musseque* first, running into the captain's house and calling out for Mrs Domingas, shouting and screaming that Mr Viriato's goat was trying to kill Xoxombo.

But Carmindinha and the rest of the family don't accept that version of events. Angry and sad, Carmindinha says that Xoxombo was still a little boy and was trying to protect *Espanhola* from the billy goat with his own body, and that's how he got injured by the horns, covered in gashes and gored by two deep holes.

The old captain raced off – old as he was, there was no one who could keep up with him. Everyone else from our *musseque* thronged around Mrs Domingas, who clung trembling to Carmindinha as they followed him up to the baobab tree. By the time they got there the boy was lying on the ground unconscious. The other boys stood around dumbfounded, not knowing what to do. Bento Abano knelt beside Xoxombo, raised his son's head and slapped his cheeks gently, trying to wake him. But blood poured from his wounds and trickled out of his mouth every time he breathed, staining his father's shirt and arms.

The evening sun had already gone and now the sky was

red like Xoxombo's blood. A light wind blew, carrying with it the wailing and sobbing of the women standing around them. Everyone stood there paralysed watching the old captain wipe away the blood. It was Zeca Bunéu who knew what to do. We all watched him run off through the grass like lightning, leaping like a goat to dodge the rubbish. It was only later on, when the ambulance arrived with its siren wailing to take Xoxombo to the Central Hospital, that we realised he'd run all the way over to the bakery where my father was working and asked him to telephone the hospital.

That evening, everyone stayed for a long time with Mrs Domingas and the girls, consoling them and telling them there was nothing to worry about – Xoxombo would be back home soon. It wasn't until ten o'clock that the captain reappeared. His wrinkled old face was like a dead man's and he didn't say a word, scarcely looking anyone in the eye. We could tell things were bad. Xoxombo had to stay in hospital.

For three weeks we went to see him every day. Dona Branca – we always called her 'Dona' rather than Mrs, just like Dona Eva and Dona Guilhermina – and her husband the shoemaker went with Zeca Bunéu, his hair carefully combed. My stepmother took me, scrubbing behind my ears and complaining about the ink that wouldn't wash out from my fingers. Carmindinha came with her perpetually sad smile which I liked so much while Tunica was her usual upbeat self. The old captain, thinner and older, was deeply affected by his only son's injuries while his wife, trusted in the will of God, as she put it.

Biquinho came all the way over from Bairro Operário where he was living now, and even Antoninho and Nanito brought sweets. Only Zito couldn't come – he was back in jail again.

But the horns of the old goat had pierced deep into his lung, and Xoxombo didn't pull through. And so one long, sad night, our friends came from all around and we sat in vigil. I think that was the night I held Carmindinha's hand for the first time and Mrs Domingas, silently crying, gave a smile of approval. The only thing I know for certain is that the first soft, terrified kiss I gave her was behind the bougainvillea at the gate of the old cemetery that drizzly day we carried Xoxombo, dear companion to all our fun and games, to his grave.

*

And so the nickname was born. When people who lived further away from the *musseque* heard the story, they chuckled to themselves, made fun of it and said our group of boys had even stooped to messing around with goats. From then on they started referring to our dead companion as Xoxombo the Goat-Shagger.

So that's the story. I'm sorry if I didn't tell it properly. I know Xoxombo will forgive me – the only reason I'm telling it like this is to do justice to his memory.

As for you, Carmindinha, when it came to that argument about the sewing course, it was your mum who knew best. Your dad, wistful old Captain Bento Abano, never really accepted the fact. Well then, Miss Mindinha, teacher of dressmaking at the Regional Association, who I'm meeting today at the gate of the Alto-das-Cruzes Cemetery where our dear friend, your brother, Xoxombo the Goat-Shagger, is buried and where he continues to flourish, am I right or am I wrong?

II

There's a mark that won't go away where the wasp bit him, that time during the rains. It's just above the knee and Zeca's always showing it off. But he hides the other one, the one he got from Nanito, the policeman's son. His excuse is that he'd have to pull down his shorts, but everyone knows it's because he doesn't like being teased. Fair enough, it's not nice having to show people a lump of lead in your backside, but then he's only got himself to blame – after all, he's the one who likes making up stories. In any case, it didn't happen quite the way he says – every time he tells it Zeca always exaggerates, and when you look into it more closely no one can tell where the truth ends and the lies begin.

1

It was a day that started out badly.

Not even five o'clock, it was still pitch dark in the *musseque* when all the fuss began. The shouting came from Albertina's, so at first none of the neighbours rushed to get up and see what was going on. They were used to it – every time she got herself a man, it always ended with him beating her up. Always the

31

same story – he'd live there in her house for a couple of months, eat her food and drink her money, then he'd slap her around a bit and leave, suitcase in hand, never to be seen again and all because Albertina said she was feeling lonely and wanted a baby. Every time she asked, there'd be one of those fights.

That day, as morning broke, the noise was louder and different – the shouts turned into moans and the neighbours began to pay more attention, coming out of their houses and gathering around her hut, feeling worried as well as curious. Albertina had been going around whispering cheerfully that she was two months' gone – she'd already confided in Mrs Domingas and Don'Ana, who'd both been mothers for ages, and had even spoken to Dona Branca, Zeca's mum, whose first reaction was that women who sleep with so many men shouldn't be having children at all. The women kept her secret to themselves and only a few of the older girls found out. So that's why they were all so concerned, fearing the worst.

Poor Albertina was curled up on the bedroom floor writhing around like a big thick snake, and there was blood pouring down her legs, staining her slip and the cement floor. Don'Ana rushed in and lit the lamp, while the other grown-ups shut the door to make sure none of us boys or girls could see anything. All we could hear were moans and low voices, and other sounds we couldn't really make out, then the sound of them lifting Albertina into her bed. They wouldn't even let us peek later on when they put the big fat white woman on the back of the fire engine.

All the fuss at daybreak was the subject of much discussion over breakfast, before the men headed off to work and the kids went out to play. Then, as they began their daily chores of washing, cooking and cleaning, the women said no more about the matter. But as they washed and cooked, they thought sadly about poor Albertina, who just wanted a baby but only ever seemed to end up in trouble. Young Carmindinha and Tunica, drumming their water cans like they were in a carnival band, had already headed off to fetch the water and from Mrs Domingas's house came the sound of her singing as she slapped the washing against the tub. That's when Zeca Bunéu turned up to play and found his three friends deep in discussion about all the goings-on.

'You don't believe me?' said Xoxombo. 'My sister saw it with her own eyes. Completely starkers, curled up on the floor. And her tummy was all black and blue like a whole battalion had marched all over her with their boots on!'

Biquinho wouldn't believe him, so little Xoxombo kicked him with his bare foot to show him what he meant. Okay, so Mr Américo really was a soldier, but real men just shouldn't do things like that.

'I'm telling you. Seems she already had his baby in her tummy and he didn't want…'

'So she was completely naked, you say?' interrupted Zito, smirking from ear to ear.

'Bloody hell, Zito! You and your dirty mind! Just shut up, will you?'

They paused for a second and Zeca jumped in to say that he was the only one who really knew – he'd seen Albertina with his own eyes writhing around on the floor, and her face had been as white as a sheet when they'd put her on the fire engine. He started with his usual storytelling routine, but then he turned serious, saying that a man who kicks a woman is no man and even if she's everyone's woman it makes no difference.

Sitting on the ground sucking ripe *gajajas* from the tree, time slipped by with nothing to distract them from the subject of Albertina and the mystery of what was wrong with her. Everyone chipped in with their opinions, but nobody really knew anything and so they just ended up going round and round in circles.

'Xoxombo! Xoxomboaaay! Get over here!'

Her housecoat hanging loosely over her heaving bosom, Mrs Domingas was standing in the doorway, angrily calling for him. The boy jumped up, dropped the slingshot into Zito's lap and ran over. Zeca Bunéu, Zito and Biquinho stayed where they were, watching. They knew that summons well – if she'd heard him talking about Albertina naked, he was probably in for a beating. He just wasn't careful, that Xoxombo – no matter how much they warned him, he just wasn't. Now he'd be sorry! The thwack of the wooden spoon, the youngster's cries and Mrs Domingas's angry voice reached them under the tree.

'*Aiuê, aiuê, mam'etuê! Nakuetuéé!*' he bawled.

'You rude boy! There – that'll teach you!'

They heard the sound they all knew so well of her wooden spoon hitting his hands and his backside and Xoxombo bleating like a kid goat. Mrs Domingas lashed angrily at him with hands and tongue, and they could hear the boy running around inside the house, tripping over things. Her scolding voice and Xoxombo's sobbing put the fear of God into his friends. Mrs Domingas flung open the door and shook her fist at them.

'You rude, rude boys! And that white *kangundu* is the worst of the lot of you – I bet you were the one who wrote those things on Xoxombo,' she shouted, pointing at Zeca. 'Nothing but white trash *ngueta* – that's what you are!'

It was always the same story. Whenever there was any kind of mischief in the *musseque*, it was always Zeca Bunéu's fault. Well, that was that – there'd be no more Xoxombo to play with that morning. And on the very day Zeca had brought his matchbox with the big red ant in it to fight Xoxombo's scorpion. Bad luck indeed!

Fed up and bored, they wandered up through the grass, practising their aim on empty bottles and losing themselves for the rest of the morning amongst the cashew and *muxixi* trees, firing off stones at the birds. It was only at about eleven o'clock, when Carmindinha and Tunica passed by on their way back down with the water cans on their heads, that they made their way gingerly round behind the house to try and speak to their friend. Sitting on a stone in the backyard, still sobbing angrily, Xoxombo was drawing patterns on the ground with a bit of palm husk. Mrs Domingas was inside with her daughters getting the lunch ready, so they called over to him.

'Xoxombo! Xoxomboaaay!'

He got cautiously to his feet, came slowly over to them and stood by the fence.

'Xoxombo, go on – lend us your scorpion to fight Zeca's ant?' Biquinho asked him.

'I'm not lending nothing to any of you lot. Piss off, all of you!'

'Now come on, Xoxombo – we didn't do anything wrong, did we? Just tell us – did we do anything wrong?'

Xoxombo shook his head.

'It was that bastard Nanito who tricked me. As soon as I find him I'll punch his lights out, just you see! Cross my heart and hope to die.'

He spat on his hand and drew a cross across his chest. But he wouldn't hand over the scorpion. No way – it was his prize fighter and it had taken him ages to catch it. When he got out that afternoon, he wanted to see for himself how his scorpion thrashed Zeca's ant good and proper.

'But Xoxombo, come on, tell me. What was it Nanito did?'

He screwed up his face and, still sobbing, started to talk in a low voice.

'Nanito was eating his avocado and he says to me, "Xoxombo, d'ya want a toy?" And so I says to him, "Yes". Then he goes and puts the avocado stone in the pocket of my school overalls. Then he says to me, "So now I'm going to draw the toy you really want here on the pocket, and by night time you'll find it inside".'

Zeca Bunéu burst out laughing. Xoxombo also wanted to laugh but his tears got the better of him.

'Oh Xoxombo, you donkey! Didn't you know that avocado stains and won't come out?'

'I forgot. Well now I know, I'll punch his face in. The bastard drew something rude.'

Glancing over towards the house, he whispered what Nanito had drawn. A squeal of laughter from all of them swept brazenly through the backyard and into the house. As they fled through the grass, they could hear Mrs Domingas shouting insults after them, while Xoxombo sought refuge in the arms of Carmindinha.

And it was that same day, which had already begun so badly, when Zeca Bunéu got the lump of lead in his backside.

2

When Nanito's father came to live here in the *musseque*, the mud-and-sticks house he rented didn't have a backyard. But behind the house there were lots of trees – guava, mango and even papaya trees – where the kids used to play. It was a big house with three rooms and a new tin roof, the same design as all the houses around here – two windows and a door at the front, two windows and a door at the back. It was between Don'Ana's house and Zito's mum's house. When he arrived one Saturday afternoon, everyone hung around to get a good look at the old police van and the two black orderlies carrying in his chairs and furniture. He wasn't the type of man who sat on straw mats and cane chairs – we could see that much straight away. The policeman, Mr Luís, didn't come over to speak to anyone, and he carried himself very straight in his neatly pressed khaki uniform, berating the two orderlies with his whip. From the way he behaved you'd think he was a big boss – until you got to know him, that is.

What with his father's delusions of grandeur and his mother always going on about their old neighbourhood, her friends down at the staff canteen, her other friends downtown and what have you, whenever the rest of them let Nanito join in their games, he was always the butt of pranks and jokes. At first he put up with it and laughed, but then he started whinging to his father and Mr Luís would come to the front door brandishing his whip.

Early one Sunday morning, the policeman started to pull apart some old barrels that had arrived the day before, and began making a fence out of the staves. The sound of his hammer blows roused the neighbours from their Sunday chores, and many came over to see what was going on.

'Just look,' they muttered to each other, 'another one of those greedy, scheming whites! As bad as the rest of them. Only been here two days and already he's behaving like he owns the place!'

It wasn't that a backyard was in itself the kind of thing to get everyone worked up about – the captain's, Don'Ana's and Granny Xica's huts all had one. But that bit of land behind the policeman's hut was where the mango and guava trees grew, and they belonged to the whole *musseque*. No one took more than they needed and even the kids respected them. Guava, papaya and mango, all just ripe for eating. Heading home at the end of the day, even other people who lived further on up would ask if they could pick a guava for the little one or even take a papaya home with them, and the answer was always the same: the trees belong to everyone and no one needs to ask.

As he drove in the nails, every blow of Mr Luís's hammer wounded the kids deeply. They felt they'd been robbed – there'd be no more playing or lying in the shade watching the birds. They said rude things about the fence and blamed Nanito.

'It was him, the sly bastard! He asked his dad!'

'So you think you can mess with us, do you? Just you wait till we get hold of you – we'll stuff your barrels where the sun don't shine!'

Zeca Bunéu was very fed up. He was the one who suffered the most, having to listen to his own dad telling Mr Luís he was quite right about the fence and that if he didn't do something he'd end up with those blacks traipsing around all over the place.

Biquinho, Xoxombo and his sisters stayed there almost the whole morning, silently watching the backyard grow, that stuck-up little Nanito handing the nails to his father and Mr Luís banging them in. Nanito's mother, Dona Eva, noticing that all the mothers were at home, came to her front door to gloat at them.

'All finished! I suppose you thought this belonged to you, did you?'

Biquinho made a rude sign with his fingers and everyone laughed. Tunica snorted in disgust.

Days and weeks went by with Dona Eva snarling at the neighbours and mocking them, while the other mothers and their kids let their tongues loose with the contempt that everyone in the *musseque* felt for 'those people'. Only Xoxombo, since he went to the same school, spoke to Nanito when he turned up wearing his sandals and carrying an air rifle, boasting that he was going to kill more *gungo* birds than anyone else. But no one else paid any attention to him and he went away again. They heard his father telling him off for wanting to play with those good-for-nothing blacks and half-castes.

Everyone in the *musseque* was divided in two camps – the captain's family and their friends on one side, Mr Luís and Antoninho's father on the other, with Dona Branca wavering somewhere in between. So no one was too surprised when, at about eight o'clock that morning when all the fuss about Albertina happened, Mr Luis came out of his house flicking his policeman's whip against his thin legs and shouting loud enough for everyone to hear, 'Today's the day I'm going to sort out that whore once and for all! Just you see. Time to make a respectable neighbourhood of this *musseque*!'

Don'Ana sucked her teeth in annoyance, cursing him in Kimbundu and, along with Mrs Domingas and the other women, taking pity on poor Albertina. Yes, it's true she was anyone's woman, but at least she was well mannered and respectful, unlike some others they could mention. And she was always kind to the little ones – that cake of hers went so fast she was always left with nothing but crumbs!

The morning passed slowly.

Then the sound of cars brought everyone back to their doorways, reckoning it was Albertina back already. But no, it wasn't her. And the boys, trapped in their mothers' angry silence, carried on aimlessly firing off pebbles under the *gajaja* tree, discussing what had happened. It was only some time after ten o'clock that they wandered up the familiar path to the place beyond the huts where there'd be flocks of *gungo* birds to take pot shots at.

In this business of the backyard, what upset Zeca most were the *pitangas*. No one else was as crazy about *pitangas* as he was. He'd even start eating the green ones, and he could strip a tree in seconds. But it was more than that. Some afternoons he'd change, become a different person. Not the cheeky kid any more that everyone in the *musseque* knew. Sitting up on the wide, raised stoop outside his house, he'd swing his legs and talk to himself, not even wanting to play. He'd look over at the guava trees, watch the afternoon breeze rustling through their leaves, smell the hot sand sweating in the morning sun and enjoy just sitting there watching people hurry by.

At times like those he'd get really angry if anyone disturbed him. We realised that what he liked was watching people, lots of people, and even more than that he liked watching the fruit trees, the fat drops of rain falling on zinc roofs and sand, and the early evening bats nibbling at the guavas and papayas. Or sometimes he'd lie under the trees on his back for seven or eight hours at a time, just looking up at the stars. That's why the whole business about the backyard hurt him so much.

And as for missing his *pitangas*, well, you didn't even dare mention them. During these afternoons of his, we'd go to watch Zeca rub his hands over their smooth leaves and gently clean the yellowing fruit, but he would not eat them. The rest of us just stared at him like donkeys – no one could figure him out. Sometimes he'd do nothing but pace up and down under the trees, talking gibberish and flicking stones in front of him in the sand. Other times, when it was already six o'clock and people were passing by on their way home from the city, he liked to sit under a tree and watch mothers with their children on their backs, picking guavas and shaking the papaya trees. And he didn't even say anything to the bolder children who pulled some *pitangas* off the tree – he didn't complain, just smiled. Not with us, though – if any of us took *pitangas*, there'd be a fight. Biquinho and Xoxombo agreed, as did Zito, who was a bit older than the rest of us, that the *pitanga* tree was Zeca's.

It all happened just after lunch.

Even though it was the time of day when the heat invites you to lie down in the cool shade of the cassava bushes or *mulemba* trees in the yard, Xoxombo went out to meet up with Zeca, who'd been whistling for him for ages. The others were up at the baobab tree giving each other dead arms with goat horns and baobab husks, but Zeca Bunéu had stayed behind. They were going to plot their revenge on Nanito. Putting his arm around Xoxombo's shoulder, Zeca began talking in a low voice, pulling the younger boy along with him.

'Bloody hell, Xoxombo – we have to get our own back on that Nanito. You have to admit, that trick of his with the avocado was a good one!'

'But how, Zeca? Just tell me and I'll do it.'

'Hey there, hold your horses!' he laughed. 'Let's wait till his mum goes for her nap. Then when he comes out into the yard, that's when we attack. I've got it all worked out.'

They stayed there sitting on the high stoop in front of Zeca's house for a long time, discussing the plan. From far away they could hear the others whistling, summoning them to play, but they ignored them. They fixed their eyes on Dona Eva's bedroom window and waited impatiently for her to appear and close the mosquito net, like she did every afternoon. They could already hear the sound of Nanito playing in the backyard, but it was nearly three o'clock before Zeca Bunéu and Xoxombo saw Nanito's mum stick her head out and close the netting. They waited a while, letting the silence envelope the huts – even the wind stopped murmuring in the leaves. Only then was it time for them begin their silent advance.

Nanito was sitting there under the guava tree, playing with his toys. Peering through the fence, Zeca put his hand over Xoxombo's mouth and told him to keep quiet. His mischievous eyes shone with laughter. Bingo! Signalling to Xoxombo to wait, he started to climb the fence with his usual skill, like a leopard creeping up on its prey. Nanito didn't hear a thing. The first thing he knew was his head was in an arm lock and his mouth covered by Zeca's hand. Xoxombo scrambled over the fence and, with a rope made out of old cloth, bound his arms and legs. Nanito tried to shout but couldn't – Zeca, skinny as he was, held on tight. Then they gagged him with Xoxombo's handkerchief and tied him to the guava tree in the middle of the yard.

Nanito looked at them furiously, twisting and turning; they could see his swollen veins throbbing like they were about to explode. But there was no way he could escape – Xoxombo had learned those knots from the old captain. Then he began to calm down and started to sob, but the boys treated him like he wasn't there, picking all the yellow *pitangas* and stuffing their faces. They ate and ate and ate until there wasn't a single one left. Ripe ones, green ones, the lot. Zeca glanced across at tearful Nanito, bound hand and foot.

'Aw, look, Xoxombo!' said Zeca, when they'd finished eating. 'Poor old Nanito doesn't have anything to eat! We shouldn't be mean to him – let's give him something to eat!'

Looking over towards the hut – Dona Eva could appear any minute – Zeca Bunéu dropped his shorts and crapped right

in front of Nanito. Xoxombo took fright and fled – he didn't
like those kinds of pranks. Tears poured down poor Nanito's
face and he bawled in anger and shame into the handkerchief
that gagged his mouth. He wanted to break free, he wanted to
shout, but there was nothing he could do. Seeing Zeca run off
after Xoxombo through the grass up towards the baobab tree,
he gave up the fight and just let his head fall and cried his eyes
out, the furious tears of a boy who'd had a filthy trick played
on him and couldn't get his own back.

It looked like it was going to rain that evening. A crazy
wind had blown in, turning somersaults in the sand and raising
whole trees of dust and paper from the piles of rubbish hidden
amongst the grass. Doors and windows slammed shut in the
face of this ill wind, and from backyards eyes scanned the
grey clouds building over the city. But then the wind dropped,
leaving only clouds that weighed on people's shoulders, and
when the sun came out again it turned so stiflingly hot and
glaring that you had to squint to see any distance at all.

Beneath the baobab tree the others squealed with laughter,
and in their houses our mothers acted as if nothing had
happened. Everything would have been fine – one of Zeca's
greatest ever pranks – if only Mr Luís hadn't come home early.
No one saw him arrive and we only realised when he appeared
with Nanito by his side, waving his policeman's whip as he
strode into Zeca's dad's workshop, demanding to see the boy.
The assistants called their boss and, caught by surprise, Zeca's
dad came over still holding his shoemaker's knife in his hand.
Dona Eva, who had come in behind her husband, screamed
that the shoemaker was going to stab him. Then Dona Branca
appeared, crossing herself and throwing a few choice insults at
Dona Eva. That's when the real trouble began. The policeman
wanted to take Zeca down to the station – the boy had gone

too far and there was just no justification for that sort of thing. The assistants had to hold back Zeca's dad, who, by now, had got himself all worked up.

'If anyone's going to teach my boy a lesson, it's me,' he bellowed. 'Clear off back to propping up the bar – you cops are all the same!'

Then Dona Branca, in that 'if we just sit down and talk we can sort everything out' way of hers, told everyone to calm down and went over to the door to call Zeca. By then, what with all the commotion, all the kids were lurking nearby and Zeca slowly came forward scratching his head. But even Zeca Bunéu's arrival, standing up like a man but shaking like jelly inside, didn't calm the situation. Yes, he was a man now and yes, he wanted to go down to the station. But they wouldn't let him. His father grabbed him by the arm and slapped him twice; the policeman pulled him by the other arm, determined to take him away. Outside with the rest of us, their eyes glinting, Don'Ana, Mrs Domingas and the other mothers and daughters nodded sagely.

'Just leave them to it. Trouble between whites is for whites to sort out!'

They smiled to themselves at the prank Zeca had played on those rude, jumped-up whites, and inside the workshop Jacinto João told the other assistants and apprentices in Kimbundu what had happened. But the argument wasn't going to blow over quickly. The arguing, yelling, threats and insults continued and Mr Luís, puffing out his little chest, wasn't going to back down – Zeca would have to spend the night in the cells. The women, who'd calmed down by now and were trying to make peace, pleaded in vain. No, he had to sleep in the cells, even if it was only for an hour. Wouldn't do him a bit of harm. But he had to take him down – it was a matter of honour.

Except then Nanito spoiled everything.

Just when his dad let go of him to grab Zeca, Nanito took advantage of all the confusion and ran back to his house. Neither Biquinho nor Xoxombo, completely engrossed in the shouting match, saw him return with the air rifle. Everything was almost sorted and they'd almost persuaded Mr Luís to let Zeca stay – the boy had already taken a few slaps and his father was blaming it all on 'boys will be boys' and that kind of thing – when Nanito came back in. Jacinto João's shout didn't save Zeca: Nanito fired a pellet straight into his backside!

Everyone shouted and ran over as Zeca collapsed, groaning, onto the big roll of shoe leather. The rumour raced around the *musseque* that the policeman's son had shot Zeca Bunéu and the kid was going to die. A crowd appeared in front of the shoemaker's house, asking questions and shaking their heads at the boys' behaviour – what's the point of all that schooling if they just go running around like bandits killing each other?

But no, it was just the shock and the sight of blood.

Talking it over and over as they returned slowly to their houses, the mothers called their children over and smacked them, just to reassure themselves after such a scare. So that's how the evening ended – the clouds disappeared far into the distance without even a drop of rain falling, and the *musseque* savoured the fresh breeze that arrived as darkness fell.

Zeca came back from hospital – they'd had to cut open his backside to extract the pellet. It was no big deal, but it hurt a lot. Nanito only came back down from the pastures later that night, well after nine o'clock, and with the promise that he wouldn't get another beating. And when everyone had finished their dinner, they avoided going outside to chat and enjoy the cooler air as they normally would, because the day had been so full of trouble.

*

A bad luck day, as Biquinho said.

He was dead right about that. Albertina still in hospital – they said she'd be there a month and would never again have children – and Zeca Bunéu out of action on account of his wounded backside. From then on Dona Eva and her husband stopped speaking to anyone in the *musseque* apart from the shoemaker and Mr Antunes. Nanito got the worst of it – he was forbidden from coming out to play with the others and the lad stewed on his own in their precious backyard.

Zeca Bunéu couldn't sit down for quite a while. Now he had yet another story to tell and before even a week had gone by, even with his friends sitting there beside him, he was telling an entirely different version of it to his cousin from Kinaxixi. But he never showed anyone the mark on his backside.

III

'My name is Xoxombo. I only say my whole name in school when teacher asks me. Then I tell her that my mother is Mrs Domingas João and she's black. Teacher says I don't need to say that. My father is Captain Bento de Jesus Abano and he's mulatto. Teacher wants me to say mixed race but that's how I like to say it. I was born in Ingombota. I'm in third year at school and I'm nine years old. Teacher is nice to me but I don't like her. She always comes over when the other boys start making fun of me and call me Monkey-Xoxombo and things like that, but I wish she didn't. She says she feels sorry for me and it's not my fault I'm so dark and anyway my soul is just the same as everyone else's. Then she hugs me like she wants to be my mum, but I don't like her because one day I brought boiled cassava for my lunch and Antoninho, whose dad, Mr Antunes, runs the grocery store ,was eating his bread and butter and started to tease me. Teacher pulled his ears and took his bread away from him, and then she threw away my cassava and gave the bread to me. But I cried and I wouldn't eat it. I just wanted my cassava which my mum had made me for my lunch.'

That, more or less, is what Xoxombo had written in that

exercise book of his, or at least what I remember of it. There were a few more pages in his big, round handwriting describing squabbles and arguments in the *musseque*. But then he stopped writing stories and moved on to rude drawings and one day Mrs Domingas found them, laid into him with her wooden spoon, tore up the exercise book and burnt it. Except that Zeca, nosey as ever, was spying on Xoxombo getting a beating and rescued a few scraps from the stove. Some of the pages just had his silly drawings on them so I threw those ones out, but I kept the others because Xoxombo had written down the things he was thinking and, every time I read them, it makes me stop to think too.

1

Sometime later there was a very still, quiet night in the *musseque* – no wind at all, even the leaves on the trees didn't move. Albertina was still in hospital and Zeca Bunéu's parents had gone to visit cousins in Kinaxixi.

After dinner Mrs Domingas came out and sat on the doorstep watching Xoxombo, Carmindinha and Tunica running around playing. Don'Ana arrived a little later on her own. She'd already put her little girls to bed and, since she knew Captain Bento was due back from one of his voyages, she'd come over to spend the evening chatting to her neighbour and helping her pass the time until he got home.

It was a dark night – the moon, still hidden behind the water tower, didn't give enough light for their usual games. So everyone was happy to see Don'Ana arrive – the kids rushed over to her and started asking her to tell stories or riddles, as only she knew how.

Zeca Bunéu heard the commotion and went over too. He

was already on his way to bed, just as Dona Branca had instructed him before she went out. But he loved listening to stories – he knew very well he'd get a beating if he wasn't in bed by the time his father came home, but he didn't care.

I watched sadly from my bedroom window as they all gathered around Don'Ana. Mrs Domingas was fanning herself in the heat. My stepmother wouldn't let me go, saying all that stuff about ghosts and *kazumbis* was only for the blacks. Whenever she said things like that it made me think about my mum who'd passed away and I'd start crying. So I strained my ears to hear what Don'Ana was telling them, and the warm silence of the night wrapped around me.

Zeca was being cheeky and kept interrupting. 'Wow! So what's a *kamukala*, then? And what's a *di-kixi*?'

The other kids were scared out of their wits, and whenever Zeca spoke they laughed as much to shake off their own fear as to make fun of him. Only Zeca wasn't embarrassed – he just wanted to know, to join in the singing and all the rest of it. That's why, when Don'Ana finished telling her story about some girls who'd gone to get tattooed, Zeca interrupted.

'Don'Ana! Can I tell my story too, please?'

'Shush, child! Questions, questions! Children who keep asking questions get nasty surprises! Can't you just sit still and be quiet?'

But Mrs Domingas was curious and said to Don'Ana to let Zeca tell his story. Xoxombo burst out laughing and Tunica and Carmindinha started to make fun of him, but all the same he began to tell his story.

'Once upon a time there was a girl carrying a basket on her head full of cassava, sweet potatoes and chickens that she was taking to her grandmother who lived far off in the bush. On the way there, Mr Leopard jumped out and started to speak to her...'

'Shut up, Zeca!' shouted Xoxombo, laughing.

'What did you say, child? That's no way to speak to your elders!' scolded Don'Ana.

'No, Don'Ana, it's not that, really it isn't. It's just that Zeca's messing it all up. The story doesn't go like that. Teacher taught us it in school. The girl's name is Little Red Riding Hood – even I know that!'

Tunica and Carmindinha, beating their mouths with the palms of their hands, started running in circles around Zeca Bunéu, shrieking with laughter and calling him an idiot.

'*Uatobo! Uatobo!*'

But even then he wasn't defeated. No sir, not our Zeca. He turned around to Don'Ana and put on a serious face.

'But Don'Ana,' he said in his wisest voice, 'if I tell a story about a girl in a red hood being eaten by a wolf and all that, nobody's going to be able to make head nor tail of it, now are they? Are there any girls like that here in this country? No. Are there any wolves in the bush here? Of course not! But we've got leopards instead and that's why I tell it like this.'

The mothers stopped laughing and nodded solemnly in agreement, then told the other children to sit down and behave. Zeca told his story right to the end, when the hunters from the little girl's village throw their spears at Mr Leopard and kill him. Goodness but that Zeca put so many lies in his story! But everyone liked it all the same.

What with all the kids' shrieking and laughing at Don'Ana's riddles, my stepmother came and pulled me away from the window, so I didn't see when Captain Abano got back. But I stayed awake the rest of the night thinking about Zeca and Xoxombo and the things he'd written in his exercise book. There was something about Xoxombo's cleverness and Zeca's imagination that seemed almost grown-up. I also thought about those arguments between my father and stepmother, things said after bedtime when no one could sleep. Xoxombo and Zito said that their parents, too, were always going on about the prices in Mr Antunes's grocery store. Mr Antunes just shrugged and said it was because of the war, but he stopped serving kids who'd been sent by their mums to fetch things and threatened that from then on it would be cash only – no more putting things on tick.

That's how, one afternoon on the way home from school, Xoxombo got into a fight with Antoninho. Xoxombo said that Antoninho's dad was getting fat on our hunger and Antoninho replied that all our families were just ignorant blacks. His dad was a proper businessman, he said, making money out of barrel hoops, empty bottles, old tyres and scrap metal, whereas our families were nothing but lazy good-for-nothings.

Xoxombo didn't hesitate, not even for a second. He just dropped his school bag on the ground and grabbed Antoninho by the head. Antoninho pushed him away and they started fighting. The others had to pull them apart. Afterwards, Xoxombo said he'd started the fight because that morning Mr Antunes had sent him away without any white sugar or even butter. Tunica hadn't heard him tell their mum and she started asking for butter, and that's when Mrs Domingas had slapped her in the face. When Xoxombo saw Tunica crying and Mrs Domingas coming out into the backyard all upset, he crossed his heart and swore he'd fight Antoninho.

But what hurt Xoxombo most was that afternoon with the toys.

2

It was one of those really bright sunny days you only get in

December, when cicadas screech from the acacia trees and everyone's eyes are flecked red with the still, windless heat. In the shade of the *gajaja* tree just before midday, Zeca and the other boys were discussing which toys they'd probably get that afternoon, and which ones they'd really like.

'Hey, Zeca! This year we'll get our wind-up trucks, right?'

'Yeah, that's what you'll get, but they're a pile of crap,' muttered Zito, who'd been in a bad mood ever since the subject came up.

Then they argued about whether Baby Jesus was the same as Father Christmas and which one brought the presents. Zeca and Zito both insisted they were right, while Xoxombo smiled sombrely.

'*Makutu!* My dad says it's the mums and dads who leave out the Christmas presents!'

Zito agreed – his dad said the same thing. Zeca Bunéu was still resolutely sticking up for Baby Jesus, but Xoxombo said sternly, 'Just leave it, Zeca! Whatever you find in your shoe, I swear it was your dad who put it there. How on earth could Father Christmas or Baby Jesus carry around all the toys for everyone?'

Zeca muttered something to himself and dropped the subject. When he called over at lunchtime, he told Xoxombo to wait for him so they could go together. Zito left earlier – no one had given him a ticket for a toy and he was fed up with the whole thing. He'd started back at school at the beginning of the year but yet again he'd had to leave. His dad had been out of work for months and what his mum earned washing clothes just wasn't enough.

On the dot of three o'clock, Zeca and Xoxombo set off down through Ingombota and up the path to the Cazuno. The heat beat down on their backs and there wasn't a single bird, not even a swallow, in the deep blue sky, only the scorching sun. Mrs Domingas and Dona Branca stood in their doorways and, as they always did, told them to behave themselves. The two women watched them disappear into the distance, down the sandy path towards Rua da Pedreira. This year's distribution was taking place in the big gardens where the bands used to play, and the boys had set off early so as to get there in plenty of time and be sure of getting a good toy.

Along the way they met other children, also walking quickly. Some were wearing sandals, others were barefoot, but they all looked very pleased with themselves, showing off their tickets and talking about which toys they wanted. Zeca laughed and chatted, always happy at the sight of lots of people. Now and again, he shouted over cheerily to some boy he knew from school. Xoxombo, his white school overalls neatly ironed, walked pensively beside him.

'Jesus, Xoxombo! You look like you've just seen a *kazumbi*!'

'It's not that, Zeca. I'm just thinking about only getting one ticket this year.'

'Don't worry – sometimes you don't even need a ticket. Remember last year?'

Yes, last year it'd been fine. The ladies had just turned up at school and told everyone where and when they'd be handing out the toys – anyone could go. But this year it had been different – when the ladies arrived everyone got excited because they knew who they were, but they didn't talk to the kids. They just left a pile of tickets and went away. After that it was the teacher who handed them out, one to each child. So how was he going to get a toy for Tunica, then?

More and more children appeared. They came from all over Ingombota, from Mutamba, from the hospital, their sweaty feet coated in dusty red sand. Some were in their school overalls, some wore smart shorts and leather shoes. Others, who came from further up, from the other *musseques*, ran along in bare feet. The girls from Kibeba walked in line in their faded red uniforms, and their bossy old schoolmistress told them off every time they looked around and giggled, their sombre little faces brightening and their eyes sparkling as the boys jostled and teased them.

Zeca and Xoxombo climbed up the Cazuno and came to the large open space in front of the governor's palace. A big crowd was there already, surging like an ocean swell right up to the statue and pushing on towards the green railings of the gardens. Boys and girls from all the schools downtown, in their smart khaki uniforms or carefully pressed white school overalls, waited impatiently in line. Sweat ran like rainwater down the teachers' faces as they called the register, and they fanned themselves busily with their newspapers. Sometimes they had to nip to the back of the line to box someone's ears, tell off the naughty ones or smack those who'd wandered off to sit in the shade. The brazen sun beamed down, stripped of its clouds, burning everyone's heads. Keko, the son of Mr Laureano who worked for the council, even fainted, and they had to carry him into the gardens and run his head under the tap. A group of boys had turned up without any adults and were messing around, giving each other dead arms and running in and out around the lines of other children. Their shrieks and insults irritated the teachers, who muttered loudly that someone should have put a stop to those rough kids from the *musseques* coming down here amongst all the nicely behaved children.

Children lined the park railings like sparrows on telegraph wires. Everyone was whistling, calling out to the ladies inside what toys they wanted and shouting that it was time to start. There was chaos in the air and Zeca Bunéu loved it. Perched on a railing, he laughed and clapped his hands while Xoxombo just stared wide-eyed at the long tables covered in toys. There were drums, horns, cars, whistles, toy soldiers – everything. The ladies, glistening with sweat, opened more and more sacks, piling the tables with things that made the kids' eyes and mouths water.

'Just look, Zeca! They've got loads of those trucks!'

'Teacher! Miss! Keep that car for me, will you?'

'Miss! I just want that drum over there!'

By four o'clock, things were getting out of hand. Food sellers drifted through the crowd selling crunchy *mikondo* pastries, spicy *kitaba* and sticky coconut sweets. Some of the cheekier ones tried to get them for free. Mothers grabbed their children by the hand so they wouldn't get lost. Policemen in those smart white uniforms they kept for special occasions and black *sipaio* troops in their brightly polished boots appeared and blew their whistles at anyone who trod on the grass, stepped on the flowerbeds, sat down on the footpath, went near the drinking fountain, or even crossed the street.

Up above the crowds, the flowering acacias were weighed down with blue, green and white shirts, fluttering like birds. Then some of those kids began to pee on the people down below. It was mayhem – the police shook their batons at them, but they just clung to the branches like cicadas and laughed. Then they jumped down onto the lawn, slipped past the policemen and ran off into the throng of people at the gate.

That's where things were getting really crowded. Boys and girls, mothers and fathers all pushed and shoved and trod on each other, but no one would step back and the gate stayed firmly shut. A child in a blue sailor's suit squeezed by, crying and calling out for his mummy. Xoxombo and Zeca laughed at the unhappy little boy, and immediately someone started to make fun of him.

'*Aiuê, Aiuê*! The big boys are going to eat me! *Mam'etu'ê...*'

'Hey there, cry-baby! Does your mummy smack you when you do a wee-wee?'

Just then a tall man in a white suit and a lady in a green dress arrived in a big black car. The policemen began to talk nicely to the kids, asking them to move back. They seemed afraid of the man in the white suit. He stepped forward, smiled at everyone and patted the heads of the children nearest to him. His wife kissed a little girl who presented her with a bunch of flowers.

The ladies inside the gardens rushed over to open the gate, smoothing down their dresses and fixing their hair as they all tried to edge in front of each other. The policemen tried and failed to hold back the kids so that the man in the white suit could make a dignified entrance. The kids piled in, shrieking and shouting, and ran straight towards the tables, trampling the flowerbeds. Those who'd been hanging off the railings jumped down, ducked around the policemen and knocked over the plant pots as they rushed to join the scramble for the toys.

Everything went crazy. The older boys pushed the younger ones and trod on the girls' feet. The girls started to cry and tell teacher. Children screamed and shouted, punched each other and started fights. Plant pots were overturned and flowers scattered. The boldest ones, already at the front, grabbed toys and hid them under their shirts. The ladies tried to fend them off with rulers as the policemen pushed and shoved, and laid into the worst offenders.

Suddenly, in the midst of all this noise, the man in the white suit appeared behind the tables. He was very tall and everyone could see him. For a moment, it was like someone had cast a spell and everything went quiet. The wind rustled through the trees and brightly coloured, butterfly-filled bougainvillea sounded like it was laughing at us. Birds sang high above and far away there was the faint murmur of water tumbling over the fern-clad rocks down in the big pool at the bottom of the gardens.

From beyond the railings you could still make out the running footsteps and chatter of late arrivals. Up in the deep blue sky, the sun sneered at the bare feet and heads of the kids waiting for their toys. Clutching their tickets, the ones in front listened to what the man in the white suit was saying. Education, civic duty, toys, Baby Jesus. None of it made any sense. When he finished his speech, the ladies all clapped and started to throw blue, green and yellow paper streamers into the air. These curled upwards and then drifted back down through the hanging creepers, clinging to the children's arms, necks and legs and covering the whole garden with a spider's web of coloured paper.

And so began the distribution. The ladies, perspiring heavily, handed out toys all around. They smiled and scolded, but they couldn't cope with all the kids pushing up against the tables, waving their tickets, shouting out what they wanted:

'I want a horn!'

'Hey, Miss! Give me that car over there, will you?'

'What do I want a doll for? I don't have any sisters!'

Overwhelmed by all these demands, the ladies started to take toys back from some kids and give them to others. Those who'd been given them first started to cry or fight with the new owners. The ladies got flustered and shouted to the policemen to take away the children who already had their toy. The police jumped in, pulled out their batons, raised them aloft with one hand and pushed the kids away with their other hand. The kids who still hadn't got anything fled the onslaught empty-handed, while some of the others grabbed even more toys.

Zeca got separated from Xoxombo in all the commotion. He took quite a few punches and when he shouted for his friend, the only reply he got was the din of all the other children. However he reckoned that he'd only need to whistle their special *musseque* signal and they'd be sure to find each other on the way out. So he ran up to the table nearest him.

'Miss! Miss!' he shouted, 'I want a wind-up truck – just a wind-up truck, please!'

He yanked back a kid who was trying to get past him. Then he saw Xoxombo's teacher.

'Hey, Miss Candida!' he called out. 'Go on, Miss, be a nice lady and give me that wind-up truck!'

That Zeca Bunéu was as bold as brass. The teacher heard what he'd said as she walked past. She saw the boy's mischievous eyes and his wide, grinning mouth as he waved his ticket.

'But you aren't from my school, are you?'

'But I know you, Miss! Go on, Miss Candida – just give me...'

Zeca wouldn't give up. He pushed against the table and held out his arm, pleading for the truck. He'd been dreaming about that truck, filling it up with sand and gravel, vrooming it around bends, playing at being a truck driver up there in our *musseque*. Right back when they'd been standing behind the railings, he'd had his eye on that big red truck with its real rubber tyres. He reached out with his neck, fingers, even his eyes, to show her exactly which one he wanted.

The teacher looked at Zeca's face, that smiling, rascal's face beloved by everyone. The gleaming wind-up truck was right there on top of the pile of toys. But no, Zeca – you and your rotten luck! Just then, just as it was within his grasp a thin man, one of the teachers from the school in Sete, rushed over. It's already five o'clock, he said – time to hurry up. He grabbed a whistle, thrust it into Zeca's hand and took his ticket.

'That's it! Over! Scram! Huh – all these street kids coming in here. *Musseque, musseque!*' he tutted.

Zeca would have minded less if the policeman had hit him over the head with his baton. Everyone knows Zeca Bunéu isn't the kind of boy to cry, but right then there was nothing he could do to stop. The tears ran down his face like someone had turned on a tap. No sobs, just tears. Zeca felt his heart break in two. There was nothing left to fight for now, no truck, no ticket, pushed away like that by that nasty thin man just when the nice lady was going to give it to him. Cross his heart he'd have looked after that truck forever. He even thought the teacher was nice – he couldn't understand why Xoxombo didn't like her.

Hot tears streaming down his face, he left, pushed around like a punch bag on his way out. He sat down on the grass with the whistle in his hand – he couldn't go any further. Things were already quietening down and he could hear the wind rustling in the leaves again, but it wasn't laughing any more. It was talking slowly, very slowly – even the trees seemed to be feeling sorry for Zeca.

The noisy racket carried on outside the gardens – shrieks of laughter, swapping of toys, games of cops and robbers, older boys stealing from younger ones. Inside the gardens, the grass was all trampled, plants uprooted and flowers scattered everywhere – it was like after one of those windy days in the rainy season. Mixed in with everything were the white tickets, blowing around among the curling blue, green and yellow streamers. The ladies, sweating and their hair all over the place, were giving out the last of the toys to the youngest children – all that was left were the whistles, party horns and paper fans.

The early evening sun was just beginning to sink sadly behind the palace. Zeca's tears still weighed on him, and he just sat there thinking about that red truck he'd wanted for so long. He let the tears roll down his face, burnt by the harsh sun of the *musseque*, and kicked angrily at the green grass until he'd scuffed it away completely. I don't know what Zeca would have done just then if Xoxombo hadn't turned up. Oh, poor little Xoxombo! His school overalls dirty and ripped, a bruised eye, a runny nose and tears pouring down his face.

'Xoxombo! Hey, Xoxombo! Who hit you? Tell me, Xoxombo. Just you tell me right now and we'll go and get'em!'

That's what Zeca's like. When someone else is in trouble, he forgets his own problems and tries to help. Still sobbing, Xoxombo held out a crumpled party horn.

'Xoxombo! So what happened? Did they hit you?'

The boy nodded. Then, sniffing back his tears, he began to tell his story.

'Miss Teacher gave me the wind-up truck like I asked her. Then all that fuss started and a man took it off me and gave it to a white boy who said he wanted it.'

Wiping his tears on the sleeve of his dirty overalls, Xoxombo said he tried to complain, but the policeman just boxed his ears. Then he started fighting with the boy who'd stolen his truck.

'Miss Teacher came and separated us and gave me this piece of rubbish.'

He threw the toy down in disgust. Then he stamped on it furiously until it was just a shapeless hole in the ground.

*

As evening slowly fell, children made their way back home, some of them heading up to Ingombota, others going down towards Mutamba. They were laughing and teasing, showing off their toys. Zeca and Xoxombo walked with their arms around each other, not speaking to anyone. They walked very slowly through the alleyways and up the sandy tracks, Xoxombo crying sometimes and Zeca heaping insults on the man in the white suit, the teachers, the school kids, everyone. Nobody escaped his fury.

The streets were dark by the time they got back to our *musseque*. Sad, ragged, dirty and toyless. Their mothers were already cross. They'd been checking back and forth between their houses and the other children had got back ages ago. Xoxombo got a beating from Mrs Domingas, but he had no more tears to cry. He didn't even try to stop her laying into him with the wooden spoon, and afterwards, in the bedroom, it took quite a while for Tunica to lull him to sleep. As for the shoemaker's house, well, Dona Branca intervened and calmed things down. But for the next two days no one saw either Xoxombo or Zeca out playing.

They never told this story to anyone again. They threw away the cardboard trucks they'd made. One night, Xoxombo wrote in his exercise book:

'Zeca and I went to where they were giving out the toys. They gave the wind-up trucks to the white kids but not to me because I'm very black. But they didn't give one to Zeca either, and he's white. Mr Laureano's son got one. I don't understand.'

IV

There's a lot of things I still don't understand in this story about Biquinho and his family. Even with Carmindinha's help and Zeca Bunéu's imagination I haven't made much progress. Zeca's no use with a story like this where no one's misbehaving, and Carmindinha's a bit older than us so she didn't know our companion very well. On my own, I can hardly bring myself to write about all the trouble when Biquinho and his family left our *musseque*. So the best thing is first of all to talk about the people themselves, and then say what happened.

Biquinho

Biquinho was a bit older than us, and when he started school he was almost fully grown. He'd been a whizz-kid in second year, Zeca Bunéu used to say – nobody could beat him at sums or tables. But he didn't make it to third year. Teacher really wanted him to, but Mrs Xica couldn't send him to school any more. Tall and skinny, and with a big head of wiry jet-black hair, there was no one as good as Biquinho for horsing around or when things got a bit tricky. He didn't even run away from the police like we did. He never said much, and the only times we saw him get annoyed was when we'd bring up all those things people in the *musseque* were saying about Mr Augusto – we always managed to find something to offend him in stuff we'd heard from our parents and neighbours. But while they all said how hard it must be for poor Mrs Xica, even calling Mr Augusto a drunkard and all sorts of other things, Biquinho said it wasn't his dad's fault and he always found a way of defending him.

'Well now,' he'd say, puffing up his chest, 'if I knew the half of what's in that book of his! I swear, Zeca, there's no man like him in the *musseque*. If you ask him, one day he'll make electricity with your comb!'

'*Makutu*! That's impossible!'

'Swear to God!'

We all said there was no way he could do that, and Biquinho said it all came from that big book we'd all seen his dad reading day after day.

'Your dads are all just thick,' said Biquinho when we made fun of his dad's book. 'It was his boss who gave him that book!'

And he carried on boasting about how the boss had given his dad the book when he'd done fifteen years' service in the workshop. But the idea didn't come from the boss, no sir. It was his dad who'd asked for the book about electricity.

So every time there was trouble in Biquinho's hut, the whole *musseque* knew how it would end: Mr Augusto thrown out of the house at the end of Mrs Xica's broom, clutching his book and staggering under the influence of the drink he'd bought down at Rascão's, issuing threats left, right and centre. We'd all chase after him and when he saw us coming, he'd stretch out his arms and point across the *musseque* sands towards the new houses.

'I'll destroy the lot of you, every last brick! That is my

curse!' he shouted, his eyes shining and his arms trembling.

'One push of a button. All gone!'

Biquinho would go up to him, close to tears, and when he saw his son like that, Mr Augusto would stop his ranting. He'd sit down with the book on his knees, pull his son's head towards him and curse himself in Kimbundu.

'*Ai mon'ami, mon'ami, a-ku-vualele uaxikelela, a-ku-vualele uaxixima.* Ah, my son, my son – when a man is born black, he is born wretched.'

Later on, as we all sat around, he'd pull out a stub of a pencil and start drawing machines and circuits and dynamos. He said he was going to destroy the city, the workshop in Bungo and all those new houses that were springing up everywhere on top of the huts they were pulling down.

Everyone in the *musseque* had already heard these threats of Mr Augusto's. Many people said someday they'd come and carry him off to the Hospital da Caridade where the crazy people went or, even worse, to a police cell. But he didn't scare any of us kids and we'd all sit around until evening fell, listening to him talk about electricity, dynamos and divine retribution – things that startled us but which we didn't really understand. And when he headed off back home with his book we'd stay where we were, not saying a word, Xoxombo lost in his thoughts, until Zeca Bunéu exclaimed,

'*Pópilas*! Your dad's a genius, Biquinho! Just a pity he drinks all day long.'

'You lot don't know the half of it, Zeca.'

'Eh? We don't know the half of what? That your dad's completely nuts?' taunted Zito.

But Biquinho would never let anyone insult his father. So he thumped Zito and they rolled around fighting. Nobody was going to say things about his dad. Even an older boy like Zito, no problem – Biquinho would fight him. And when the fight was over he'd come out smiling whether he'd won or lost.

'Just you wait!' he'd say to the rest of us. 'One day I'll be like him, you'll see! An electrician, that's what! None of you'll ever understand it like I do – you can only read about it in your books.'

Biquinho, our silent companion, went off home. Sometimes Mrs Xica was already calling him from the door. Then the rest of us would all wander down to the lower pastures and talk over and over what Mr Augusto had said.

Mrs Xica

It's good to talk about Biquinho's mum. She was our friend – there was none of that nonsense like with Dona Eva, Dona Guilhermina or even Dona Branca. She'd always give us crunchy *mikondos* to eat, or sticky *jinguba* cookies that were always a little bit burnt. They were the ones that Dona Guilhermina, Antoninho's mum, wouldn't accept – she only paid for the good ones. Dona Guilhermina provided the sugar, peanuts and flour for Mrs Xica to make them, and then paid her in kind with food from her husband's grocery store.

Dona Guilhermina made lots of money from her business selling sweets and pastries. She herself boasted about it. At the beginning, she had only one young lad to help her, but as things expanded she was sending four employees off to sell Mrs Xica's pastries on the Calçada da Missão and around by the Coqueiros football pitch, and even all the way downtown.

Our friend was very thin from working so hard every day. She seemed more like a little girl – standing beside her, Carmindinha looked older. But when we got close enough to see her eyes, we could tell that Biquinho's mum was suffering

– they always seemed washed out somehow, with no colour or sparkle in them. Don'Ana said it was because of all the heat from the stove and the iron. Mrs Domingas said it was from the poor woman weeping so much over her useless husband. All the women felt sorry for their friend, ironing, cooking and washing clothes all day only for Mr Augusto to spend all her money down at Rascão's bar with his drinking pals.

One day, Captain Abano asked her why she didn't organise some of the kids to sell her pastries – that way she'd be earning more money. But even though Mrs Xica was quite capable of hitting Mr Augusto with her broom when she was annoyed with him, she didn't like to speak ill of her husband to other people. So she just made excuses.

'Yes, brother, you're quite right. But then there's the trays, you know – where would Augusto get the trays from?'

'*Sukuama*!' Bento swore. 'Just tell him to find any old soapbox and take it down to Zuza's workshop – easy!'

'Yes, that's true,' Mrs Xica continued, 'but then I'd need a licence from the council. There's the problem!'

Everyone knew that Biquinho's mum was trying to save the money to get the trays made and obtain the street vendor's licence, but Mr Augusto kept finding the money and spending it down at Rascão's. Some nights when her husband came home drunk after spending the whole day there, we'd hear the sounds of Mrs Xica and Mr Augusto fighting, and Biquinho crying in the middle. There'd be the thump of her hitting him with the broom and him saying over and over that he was sorry, but he never raised a finger against his wife. Even with their hut being so far away, up towards the baobab tree, the whole *musseque* could hear the poor woman's shouts and wails, crying over the money. The women and the older girls got some satisfaction from hearing all the racket, but their menfolk told them off.

So the women exchanged their knowing glances and barbed comments amongst themselves.

'*Poça*! Drinking away that poor woman's money again? It's a bad business.'

'Well, if that was my husband, I'd have him thrown in jail.'

'There's just no call for it, sister,' Don'Ana said to Zito's mum. 'That poor woman slaving over the washtub all day long and him drinking every penny she earns.'

Mrs Domingas would occasionally reminisce about the better times, back in the early days of the *musseque*.

'*Aiuê*! If you'd only known him back then, sister! His boss even used to bring him home in a car. In a car, sister! All the way up here! That was when he was working down in Bungo.'

'It's like someone's cast an evil spell on him, sister Domingas. A man like him, turn out like that?'

Don'Ana shook her head sadly.

'He and I used to be good friends and that's a fact,' Captain Abano added. 'An intelligent man like him – it just doesn't make any sense.'

The conversation turned once again to Mrs Xica – so thin and worn out now, but such a fine figure of a woman back in her days of dancing *rebitas* and *massembas*. And so the night ended with fulsome praise for both her beauty in days gone by and her hard work now at the ironing board, washtub and stove, but with never enough money to keep Biquinho in school.

Mr Augusto

Anyone who hadn't known him in earlier days wouldn't have believed that Augusto João Neto was once chief electrician in the big workshop down in Bungo.

But that was indeed the truth, as confirmed by the captain, Mrs Domingas, Zito's dad and all the other grown-ups here in the *musseque*. However, the difference between the Augusto João Neto of old and the Mr Augusto of today was so great that none of us believed them. It was only when Mr Augusto started talking, drawing his machines, showing us things from his book, making electricity with his comb and doing all sorts of other magic, that we stopped arguing about it with Biquinho.

For as long as any of us could remember being here in the *musseque*, we could remember Mr Augusto. Not always drunk, it's true, and not always talking to himself, standing with his book open in one hand pointing accusingly with the other at the new houses rising up across the sandy wasteland. Some mornings when he was a bit calmer, he'd head off downtown and Mrs Xica would say he'd gone to look for work.

One night Mrs Domingas had a long discussion about Mr Augusto with Don'Ana, who never had a good word to say about him. We listened in, wide-eyed, as she told her all about the shopkeeper's son from Funda whose father had sent him to Luanda to study for the priesthood. Bento Abano, sitting in the corner, put down his newspaper and joined in.

'Oh, he was a real scholar! He'd just turned eighteen and suddenly he left the seminary to become an apprentice in a workshop. Even today, no one knows what happened.'

'Oh, there are lots of things people had to say about that, sister – you mark my words!' continued Mrs Domingas. 'You remember my friend Santa from Coqueiros? Well, she says it was all to do with a romance with a slip of a girl who was always coming to mass with her mistress, some fine lady from the palace…'

We shifted closer, our ears straining to hear all this talk of romance, but Captain Bento only wanted to talk about Mr

Augusto's job.

'Best workman they had,' he interrupted again. 'They even put him in charge. Back in those days there wasn't a better electrician than Augusto João Neto in the whole of Luanda!'

They listened silently as he spoke of the fine qualities of that 'son of the people' as he liked to call him, of how he was praised by his bosses and respected and esteemed by the whole population.

'As God's my witness, it's the truth! It was Augusto who installed the electricity for the great exhibition when President Carmona came in '38.'

And it was still so recent that even I remembered it. It was this proof, which the captain had kept till last, that convinced all the neighbours – even Zeca's dad, who always said the blacks were no good for anything but apprentices.

One night, Xoxombo interrupted one of these conversations.

'So then, what's this book of his?'

Mrs Domingas turned around and told her son to be quiet, but then she asked her husband,

'Go on, Bento, tell them. These boys…'

With his calm, authoritative voice, Bento Abano carried on talking into the night about the young worker's dedication and the nights he spent studying all the books he could buy, until the day came when, as a reward for completing fifteen years' service, the boss gave him that great big thick book, the mystery of the whole *musseque* and a marvel to all us kids.

But the story of Mr Augusto wasn't all so clear-cut. Parts of it were full of shadows and things nobody could explain. The electrician said little and only liked talking about the ordinary everyday stuff. Leaving the seminary, quitting his job and even marrying Mrs Xica at a time when he was such an eligible bachelor – all these remained shrouded in mystery.

'No one knows for sure. One thing's certain: he was fired. The old man's son came and took over the workshop. That's when Augusto took to drink. He'd look around for other jobs, find something, get caught slacking and then get fired again. And always going on and on about those inventions of his.'

The captain's voice, with its restful seaman's lilt, murmured softly in our ears that hot, quiet night. And for all of us kids who adored Mr Augusto's stories, magic and machines, the old captain's words conjured up in our minds that tall, skinny, staggering figure, his electricity book in one hand and the other pointing threateningly across the sands.

And for Xoxombo, star pupil at the Evangelical Mission, Biquinho's dad became like one of those bearded old men in the Bible who, when the world had just begun, went around talking about the coming of the Messiah.

The Events

Λ peace that came from times gone by, which neither I nor any of the other kids remembered but which the grown-ups still talked of as they sat on each other's doorsteps at night, bound all these families together as friends and neighbours. This was despite all the arguments, grumblings, fallings-out and makings-up that sometimes threatened to spoil things but which, in the end, were the ultimate proof of that longstanding neighbourliness and friendship.

That's what they all said – Captain Bento, Don'Ana, Sebastião Domingos Mateus and even Zeca's dad, who, by then, had been living in our *musseque* for quite a while. And this peace, which we'd all taken for granted and which came with the morning mists in the cool season, with the juice of December cashews in the hot season, and with the flocks of birds and the fresh new grass of the first rains, began to be talked about with longing and regret when, creeping up through Ingombota, the bright red roofs of new houses began to peer enviously in at our *musseque*.

A sheaf of notices from the city council had been delivered to the people who lived over towards Braga. Then, months later, we saw the workmen come with their bulldozer to tear down the huts and smooth the earth flat. Those who hadn't believed the bits of paper rushed to haul their belongings out of their huts as the workmen ripped sheets of corrugated iron off the roofs and as the dried mud walls, still holding the warmth of the people who lived within them, resisted briefly before collapsing in a cloud of red dust under the force of the bulldozer. Men in brimmed hats peered through strange eyeglasses and made signals with their arms while workmen wandered around with stripy poles. Truckloads of sand and gravel began to arrive from Bungo. The peace and calm of our *musseque*, even as the bright green grass and ripening cashews basked in the January sunshine, took on the smell of engine smoke, and the evening breeze blowing in from Mussulo Bay enveloped everything in a fine cloud of dust.

Soon it was our turn for bad luck.

Of all the families in our *musseque*, only Biquinho's dad had received the piece of paper – they lived quite far away from the rest of us, up by the baobab tree over towards Braga. Mr Augusto hurled insults at the white man who delivered the notice, threatened to blow up the city council, and said he was off to find his book. But Mrs Xica came to the door, apologised and dragged her husband back into the hut before there was any more trouble. By the time the others passed by, fleeing with their children and all their belongings up beyond the sands towards Burity and Terra Nova, Mr Augusto had reappeared with his book.

'I'm not leaving this house!' he shouted, waving his arms menacingly. 'I pay my rent and no one's getting me out, even if they come and beat me!'

'Just listen, brother Augusto – you know that when it comes to the council, that's just the way things are.'

Mr Augusto opened his eyes until they were wide as a leopard's.

'Well what about my invention, then?' he snarled. 'I only have to press the button...'

Mrs Xica kept trying to look for somewhere else to live, but that meant there'd be no one at home to do the work, so there'd be no food to eat. We could see the bulldozer pacing across the grass, its yellow teeth ripping up everything in its path, and we warned Mrs Xica that sooner or later it was going to reach her and then it'd be like with Mrs Fefa who was nearly killed inside her own home.

'White man has no heart, sister. They'll turn up and pull everything down, even with you inside!'

Mrs Xica wouldn't believe any of it – when the time came, she reckoned she could go and speak to the man driving the bulldozer and ask him to let them stay. Their little hut was far away from all those new houses – no one was going to need it. Mrs Domingas came to give her some advice and Captain Bento went to speak to Mr Augusto to tell him to go and see Mr Laureano down at the council, but it was difficult to find a time when he wasn't fighting drunk.

Time went on, the ripened cashews fell from the trees and the grass turned brown. Biquinho left school and went to work in the workshop. Zito was thrown in jail, after some trouble about the pastry seller's money. It was the school holidays, the sun was beating down and when the bright yellow, brand-new bulldozer reappeared racing through the sands, belching black smoke and threatening everything in its path with its glistening teeth, Zeca Bunéu, Xoxombo and I had been playing *quigozas*. It'd been a pretty tiring game, so when afternoon came, we gave up and sat under the *gajaja* tree, talking about all the usual things. It was a beautiful day and Zito's canaries were singing in their cage. A good rain had fallen during the night, dampening the red earth, freshening the air and rinsing the branches of the trees up in the pastures. You could smell the bougainvillea, jasmine and cassava bushes even from inside the huts. By then it was already four o'clock, the sun had lost its fire and it turned into a fine evening.

Early the next morning, the bulldozer was back, its screeching voice and belching fumes polluting the air even up where we were sitting under the tree. Mrs Xica heard the noise and came to the door, but seeing that it was still some distance away she went back inside to make Biquinho's cassava porridge. It was only after her son had left the house that she woke up Mr Augusto, still asleep on his mat.

'The bulldozer's here.'

'So? What's it to do with me?'

'Oh, for God's sake, man – don't talk nonsense. Don't you understand? It's come to throw us out!'

Mr Augusto yawned and rolled over. Mrs Xica, her heart sinking, went outside to seek the advice of her neighbours. Mrs Domingas thought the best thing would indeed be to go and talk to the man in the bulldozer to find out what was happening.

'What on earth's that husband of yours for, sister? What's he for? For goodness' sake! He's the one who should go and talk to the white man!'

And when Mrs Xica came back out, feeling somewhat

reassured, Xoxombo, who'd been listening in on the conversation, came and warned the rest of us. But nothing more happened for the rest of that morning. The bulldozer was still working up where the big cashew trees were, and it was only its noise and fumes that invaded the hut.

At eleven o'clock Mr Augusto finally got up and went out without saying a word to his wife. Mrs Xica stood in the doorway, her heart sinking again as she watched her husband stumble off through the long grass. With the other eye she could make out the yellow monster gnawing at the trunks of the old cashew trees. It was only after four o'clock that it finally happened. The bulldozer turned back down the hill towards Makulusu and hurtled at full speed across the grass and sand, swallowing giant grasshoppers and startling the birds, its sharp metal teeth glinting in the sunlight. Mrs Xica was sitting on the doorstep taking a break from the washtub when the sound of the engine reached her ears. She stood up and her thin body trembled under the onslaught of the noise.

'*Aiuê, Ngana Zambi'ê!*' she cried. 'Lord, have mercy! My time has come!'

Without even closing the door behind her, she grabbed the piece of paper the white man had delivered all that time ago and started to scream, '*Nakuetu'ê!* Help, neighbours, help! We are ruined!'

Xoxombo and Zeca heard her first. Antoninho came down from the *gajaja* tree and warned the rest of us, 'Look! Biquinho's mum is on her way over here – and she's running!'

By the time Mrs Xica reached the captain's hut, Don'Ana, Dona Branca, Zito's mum and all of us kids were already there waiting for her.

'*Aiuê, lamba diami!* I'm done for now – the bulldozer's coming!' she wailed.

'Calm down, Xica! Come on now, pull yourself together.'

'I can't, I just can't, sister. What am I going to do now? There's no one here to help me.'

Biquinho's mum shook her head from side to side and tears streamed from her weary eyes. Mrs Domingas came in and put on her sandals. Standing beside Carmindinha and Tunica, she said to the rest of the women,

'Whoever wants to can come and help. If Bento was here, he'd go and speak to the white man. Maybe he'll agree to wait.'

'Come on, let's go!'

The group of women set off along the track through the grass – Mrs Xica in the middle, her tears already drying, and the kids running along behind in awe of the bulldozer. Standing in their doorway, Dona Branca and her husband the shoemaker watched them go.

'Leave them to it. Nothing to do with us,' he said to her.

'But the poor woman's going to be thrown out in the street! You could at least go and speak...'

'They were warned a long time ago,' he said, cutting her off.

When the group arrived, the driver had already climbed down from the bulldozer. The machine stood staring silently at the hut while one of the workmen poured a can of petrol into the tank. The boys ran over and Mrs Xica edged forward towards the hut. The driver was walking around inside the hut and they could hear his voice calling out, 'Anyone home? Bloody negroes...'

Mrs Domingas came forward with her neighbour and collided with a short, fat man coming out the door.

'Hey, you!' Mrs Xica called out. 'So you think you can just walk into someone's house without so much as a by-your-leave, do you? Bloody whites. No manners.'

'You've no right taking advantage of people like that,' said Don'Ana, shaking her fist at him.

The man looked at the group of women standing there defiantly, some holding children by the hand, and changed his tone. 'It's not my fault. I knocked and nobody answered.'

'And so you just walked right in, is that it? Made yourself at home?'

'Okay, that's enough. Who's the owner?'

Mrs Xica came forward.

'Where's your husband?'

'He's not here.'

'Didn't you get the piece of paper telling you to leave before the end of the month?'

'We got it. But we couldn't find anywhere to move to.'

The driver smiled sarcastically. 'Rubbish! You mean in three months you couldn't find another hut? Was it a palace you were looking for?'

'It's true, mister!' interrupted Don'Ana. 'We helped her look.'

'Shut up! You're all a bunch of liars.'

Mrs Domingas, Don'Ana and Zito's mum kept on trying, but the man wouldn't give in. He replied that he had his orders, the council had given them notice and he was going to pull down the hut, right now. A murmur of protest rose from everyone gathered around; it grew louder and a few voices shouted insults in Kimbundu, calling him *ngueta*, *kangundu* and the other words we used for mean, low-class whites.

Mrs Xica left the group of women and ran over to the house, blocking the door with her thin body. Caught by the wind, her dress flapped like a flag. 'Listen here, you jumped-up *kangundu*, you think you can make fun of us just because we're women, is that it? Well, if we weren't, we'd bust your guts!'

'Yeah, it's a pity her husband isn't here. You picked your time, didn't you?'

The driver of the bulldozer looked astonished at the angry women, at Biquinho's mum brandishing her broom from the doorway and at his own workmen smirking behind the bulldozer, whispering to each other in Kimbundu.

'I'll give you half an hour for you to clear your belongings,' he announced. After that, I've got my orders. Just make sure the hut's empty by then.'

'Just you come over here, you little piece of white shit! I'll knock your block off!'

Mrs Xica certainly wasn't behaving like the lady we used to know. All the veins in her neck and arms were sticking out and she waved her broom around menacingly. Some of the women muttered insults while others pleaded for a few more days for her to find another house. The driver of the bulldozer, sweating profusely, looked from one to the other but wouldn't give in. Then Biquinho's mum, thinking there was nothing more to lose and screaming like a madwoman, hit him with the broom. That's when he finally did something, grabbing her round the waist and wrenching the broom from her grasp. Don'Ana and her other friends ran over, the children started to taunt him, his own workmen clapped their hands in glee and, within a split second, the driver found himself surrounded by a menacing group of clenched fists and screaming voices. He shouted above the noise, then, one by one, pushed the women out of the way and tried once again to convince them.

'It's not my fault! For Christ's sake, I'm just following orders! I have to pull down the hut today. Tomorrow the mayor's coming to inspect the site. Shit! Look, just take your belongings out of the hut, otherwise I'll have to pull it down with everything inside.'

Mrs Xica threw herself on the ground crying in anger, beating her hands and feet on the sand, cursing Mr Augusto.

'What's the point of having a husband? Just to sleep with and have babies? That useless, worthless drunk!'

The other women helped her up, brushed off the dust and took her into the hut. We could hear her wailing and crying from outside and even the driver's workmen stopped laughing. The driver, swearing angrily, came back up to the bulldozer and chased us away. He switched on the engine, filling the air with foul-smelling black smoke while the women and girls began to bring out all the furniture from the hut. We ran over to help as well and everyone set to work like a trail of ants.

It was painful to see everything scattered over the ground like that – things we all knew and which had their place, neatly arranged, inside the house. Exposed to the afternoon sun, they looked dirty, broken and worthless. Inside the shade of the house they'd been objects that said something to each of us – the big clay jug said cool, fresh water, the tin mug said thick, sweet *kikuerra*, and the baskets made from tree bark said fine white flour for making pastries to sell, or coarse *musseque* flour for our own bread. But now, jumbled up on the sand, it all looked more like a rubbish tip.

Out came Mrs Xica and Mr Augusto's bed mats. Then Biquinho's rusty old iron bed where we'd fought so often, but which now just looked like a piece of scrap metal, still with its white sheet where the bedbugs were beginning to stir, startled by the sun and noise. Then came the food-stained table and the chairs that had long since lost their varnish. Finally, Mrs Xica and the other women carried out the water butt, stove and floor mats.

We all felt very sad seeing all these things – even Biquinho's little wooden trunk, to which Don'Ana added his school bag, his slate and his second year schoolbook. The driver had turned off the engine and was behaving with a bit more respect now, and his workmen were helping take things out of the hut. Mrs Xica emerged with that old framed Sacred Heart of Jesus and the portrait Biquinho had drawn of President Carmona, and threw them both on the pile.

It had already gone five o'clock, the sun had lost its heat and a handful of laundrywomen who'd just finished work stopped to ask what was happening and lament the misfortunes of life, and then went on their way.

Once everything had been removed the workmen pulled out the doors and windows, which made the hut itself look sad, and Mrs Xica burst out crying again. Biquinho had been born there, and she'd lived there so long she couldn't believe that now it was really over. The bare walls revealed where pictures had hung, where flies had been swatted, where nails had been hammered in and where the rain had seeped through. When the workmen pulled off the corrugated iron roof, the walls turned ugly, old and naked in the unforgiving daylight.

We all fell silent. We could hear the wind in the trees, the birds sweeping low, people's voices far away, the sweating grunts of the workmen and the crash of the corrugated iron sheets falling to the ground. The women and older girls, pensive and sad, were sitting on the piles of scattered belongings and Biquinho's mum wept silently.

'Right! Time to go! Take what you can carry and scarper!'

The driver's coarse, threatening voice broke the silence, screeching almost like a crow's. The bulldozer roared back into life, belched out smoke and lurched towards the hut, huffing and whining. They could hear the walls resisting, gently moaning under the pressure as if the red clay and reeds were clinging on to each other. Then, with a wrenching noise, bits of clay and reed flew up in the air and clouds of red dust, carried by the sea breeze, engulfed the yellow bulldozer as it turned in retreat, making the driver cough furiously. The house that had given birth to Biquinho, our silent companion, was now only fragments of half-standing walls, which, with just a few more gentle nudges from the bulldozer, came tumbling down. Nothing remained standing; the battle was lost.

The mothers and daughters rushed back over to shake the dust from the furniture and move it further away while the bulldozer finished its work. The boys watched wide-eyed as the machine, like some evil spirit, levelled the ground and cleared everything in its path. It was the ruler of everything and nothing could stand in its way.

Mrs Xica, Mrs Domingas, Zito's mum and the other women began to gather everything together to take it over to Bairro Operário. That's where Biquinho's mum would go – her sister lived over there and still had some space in her hut. Mrs Xica would ask her sister to let the three of them share a room there. It wouldn't be so bad for Biquinho who'd be nearer his new job, just a short walk down through the clay pits to the workshop in Boavista.

'So now then, sister, how are you going to carry all this furniture?'

'I haven't a clue. I suppose I'll wait for Augusto. For Christ's sake, that man needs to get a grip!'

'*Sukuama*!' cursed Mrs Domingas. 'If you hang around waiting for that drunkard, you'll end up sleeping right here on the ground with all your belongings around you. Best thing would be to ask the white man with the bulldozer.'

'What? There's no way he'll agree.'

'Well, we'll try asking him nicely. He's got a trailer over

there, under the cashew tree – I can see it from here.'

'Go on, you ask him, sister. I can't, not now – I'm too angry. Just you wait till I get my hands on that good-for-nothing drunk…'

Mrs Domingas carefully pulled her dress fabric up over her shoulder and walked up to the tree where the driver was standing beside the parked bulldozer, wiping his hands.

'What now? More complaints?'

'No, it's not that. Just listen to me, please. This woman here is my friend. Her husband is sick. You know these things are too heavy for the poor woman to carry all on her own…'

'And?'

'If you would be so kind, could you take the heavy things in your trailer? She'd be very grateful.'

The driver looked at Mrs Domingas in utter amazement.

'What? Are you crazy or something? The trailer belongs to the council!'

He stood there thinking for a while, looking at Mrs Domingas and the other women, then at the furniture scattered over the sand. Everyone's eyes were fixed on him. He sensed their expectations and, without saying a word, walked slowly over to the cashew tree and returned with the trailer.

'Hey you – João! Toko! Load the furniture onto the trailer. Make it snappy!'

The women thanked him profusely, and Mrs Xica even apologised for the broom – but, you know, my husband's sick, my son's still at work and what's a poor woman to do on her own?

'Okay, okay. I've heard it all already.'

They loaded up the trailer and everyone said goodbye to Mrs Xica, wishing her all the best, promising to tell Biquinho and Mr Augusto, and also Dona Guilhermina on account of the pastry business. She started clambering into the back of the trailer, but the driver waved to her to come and sit up in front with him. As they set off, people called out their farewells and a few of us couldn't resist the temptation to hitch a ride on the rear bumper.

'Oh, sister!' said Mrs Domingas to Don'Ana as they walked back to their huts. 'At least some of those whites behave decently. If it wasn't for him, the poor woman would be sleeping there on the ground!'

Don'Ana wasn't having any of it – she said that if they behaved decently, they wouldn't pull down people's huts without providing new ones. The other women changed the subject and blamed Mr Augusto.

'It's all the fault of that man of hers. They had plenty of warning.'

'Well it's not her fault, that's for sure.'

As the evening sun fell, lots of people making their way home along the same path they used day after day were surprised to find the hut gone and asked what had happened. Zeca Bunéu told them the whole sorry tale, imitating the bulldozer as he did so. Xoxombo joined in too, and slowly the people carried on up the hill, discussing with each other or thinking quietly to themselves about what it all meant. That very morning, heading down to work, they'd seen that woman standing in her doorway skinning ox tongue, and now what? Not even a trace of the house remained. Only a reddish stain beside the path, a few broken reeds and some lumps of clay.

We sat there talking it over and clambering over the bulldozer under the watchful eye of one of the workmen. Mrs Domingas had asked us to tell Biquinho when he got back from work, or Mr Augusto whenever he turned up. It was almost night time when our silent companion appeared. We didn't need to say anything. He turned away from us, kicked at a few lumps of clay and just stood for a long time on the spot where his bedroom had been. Then, without a word to any of us, he walked over to the bulldozer, spat on it, hurled every swear word he knew at it, and started to cry softly.

'Time to go, Biquinho. Your mum's gone to Mama Lolota's house, over in Bairro Operário.'

But Biquinho wouldn't go. He sat down on the ground, stopped crying and started talking to us about the hut, the bulldozer, the piece of paper.

'I told dad to get a move on about finding another house.'

Happier with the turn the conversation was taking, we could feel night falling and soon there were only his words in our ears. The moon hadn't yet risen and Biquinho was telling us that his boss had given him a raise, that he really liked being an electrician and that he was going to ask his dad for the book, so he could study more.

'But how, Biquinho? You can hardly read.'

'True, Zeca. But this way I'll learn reading and electricity at the same time!'

Later on, as we passed Rascão's bar on our way up to the baobab tree, we heard a familiar voice ranting on about machines destroying houses and making all sorts of threats, and we realised why Biquinho hadn't gone yet. Our friend was waiting for his father, but he asked us to go on home.

Xoxombo said goodbye, promising that he and Zeca Bunéu would go over and play on Sunday, but Biquinho shook his head.

'No, Xoxombo. I'll be living far away now, and on Sunday I want to study.'

With our arms around Xoxombo, and with Zeca Bunéu whistling to frighten off his fear of the dark, the three of us made our way home through the long grass. As we passed the baobab tree, the moon was already rising behind the water tower. We looked at where Biquinho's house had been. The yellow bulldozer peered back at us from under its tarpaulin. The workman who was minding it had already lit a fire to cook his dinner. In the pale moonlight and by the flickering light of the fire, we could see Biquinho sitting on the ground and Mr Augusto standing on the broken lumps of clay and reed, one hand holding his book and the other pointing sternly down towards the sands.

'*Pópilas*, Zeca! Look!' exclaimed Xoxombo. 'They look just like those old men in the Bible! You know – the ones who go around preaching about the wrath of God!'

I felt Zeca Bunéu pull me closer to him and, whistling even louder, we returned home without saying another word.

The Truth about Zito

V

On that misty June morning in a year I can hardly remember, when I arrived in the *musseque* clutching my father's hand, the first person I saw was a tall, strong boy leaning against the wall of my stepmother's house. He watched me suspiciously and curiously as he rubbed his bare foot against the corner of the wall. He was hiding something cupped in the palm of his hand, but he waved to us, watching my face. His eyes were small and had a way of not looking straight at you.

'Well, hello there, Toneta's very own St Anthony!' replied dad with a grin.

The lad tossed aside his cigarette stub like a grown-up and, without the slightest hint of fear or shame, swore back loudly,

'Yeah, well, St Anthony can go fuck himself.'

My jaw dropped. Dad told me the boy's name was Zito.

1

When the door opened and Carmindinha rushed in, dripping water all over the kids sitting on the mats, they all looked up at the thick, fat ribbons of water pouring from the grooves in the corrugated iron roof, shaking in the wind. Cool air and the fresh smell of wet earth wafted in through the open door, filling the hut and mingling with Carmindinha's laughter and Mrs Domingas's scolding.

'Be careful, girl! Letting the rain in like that...'

The rain had been falling since ten o'clock. The water drummed on the tin roof like the big fat fingers of a demented percussion player, and Zeca Bunéu and Xoxombo, running around naked in the backyard, threw their heads back and let the clouds fill their open mouths. Zeca had come round to the captain's house as soon as the first drops of rain began to fall – Dona Branca wouldn't allow him to play the shower game at home and it was only in Xoxombo's backyard that they could get up to their favourite trick: filling their mouths with water, pretending to drink, and then standing perfectly still under the big, warm raindrops.

'Hey! Look at us!' they shouted over to the other kids. 'It's a magic spell! We drank some water just now and look – we're already peeing!'

The streams of water trickled down their chests, funnelling together beneath their tummies in a great jet of water that only those two boys with their endless tricks and games – not to mention their special knack of contorting their shoulders, chest and stomach – could manage.

Of the three kids on the mat, only Zito wasn't playing. He'd been silent and brooding all morning, watching Tunica's expert fingers beat Biquinho at the pebble game. Even when it started raining he didn't want to go outside with Zeca and Xoxombo. Looking at Tunica he mumbled, 'I'm a grown-up now – I don't do that yard thing any more.'

He was always muttering about something or other, and his old habits of swearing were getting even worse.

'*Pópilas*, Zeca!' exclaimed Xoxombo, outside in the rain.

'What's wrong with Zito, today? He looks like he's seen a *kazumbi*!'

Zeca Bunéu laughed, but the warm rain was falling heavily and he didn't reply.

It's true – Zito was no longer the boy they used to know. Yes, he'd always been the older one, but only old enough to teach them how to use a catapult, how to pull branches off the *mulemba* trees and how to cheat at cards. But these days he kept himself to himself and the only thing he seemed to want was to be near Carmindinha, watching over her like a rooster and either saying nothing or just talking a load of rubbish. Or sometimes when Toneta, old Granny Xica's granddaughter, was coming home from work at six o'clock, he'd sneak out and climb up into Xoxombo's *mulemba* tree where no one could see him.

'Xoxombo, you remember that cousin of Zito's?'

'Yes, I remember – the one who runs the print works up in Cidade Alta?'

'Yes, him. Well he's the one who came and ruined our Zito.'

'How's that then?'

The cousin had arrived one hot Sunday to help Zito's dad, Sebastião Mateus, fix the roof on their hut because the rain was coming in. They'd worked all morning and then they'd talked and talked long into the evening. Later on, Zito said the cousin had told him lots of things but he wasn't going to repeat them because the rest of them were all still babies. He also showed them the cigarette his cousin had given him to smoke. As time slipped by with nothing to do but wait for the rains to end, bit by bit Zito told them the cousin's story: he'd slept with a girl from Sete and, what's more, he'd promised to take Zito there, because Zito wasn't a boy any more.

'Bloody hell, Zito! Take you to do what?'

Zito did all that grown-up stuff of his and said nonchalantly, 'To sleep with her, of course!'

Biquinho burst out laughing.

'You can't, Zito. You're still a boy – you can't make babies!' said Zeca.

'Hey, so you only sleep with a woman when you want to make a baby? For Christ's sake, Biquinho, you can be a real idiot sometimes!'

'But it's true, Zito! Men sleep with women so they can make babies!'

Zito told Zeca to shut up. Nine-year-olds like him had no place in a grown man's conversation.

'Anyway, my cousin says I'm a man now!'

To Zeca, still too young, the cousin's story didn't make much of an impression. But from that moment on, Zito changed. There was no more chatting and, come six o'clock, he'd disappear and no one would see him again. Xoxombo even ran over to the *mulemba* tree, but he wasn't there. One day Biquinho told them he'd followed Zito up to the big tamarind tree and seen him spying on the women peeing below.

'Swear to God and hope to die!'

'But spying on what? How's he going to see anything beneath their skirts?'

Apparently Zito had even climbed down from the tree to look at the damp hole in the ground and, one day when it was already dark, Biquinho had even seen him sniffing it.

This story of Biquinho's kept coming back to mind now that Zito was hell bent on hanging around Carmindinha. He watched hungrily as she passed by, her dress wet from the water cans, her little nipples poking through. And then, when six o'clock came, Zito would disappear, making excuses that he had to go and help his mum.

But no one, not even Biquinho who was older than him, really knew what was going on inside Zito's head. He'd been suffering ever since that time his cousin had told him about the girl from Sete. For days he could think about nothing else, the words danced around in his head like little figures from the drawings in his reading book. And Carmindinha, passing by in front of him with her wet dress riding up above her knees, kept reminding him of his cousin 'inviting him to be a man', as he put it.

He'd already told Biquinho he was going to stop hanging around with those little boys Xoxombo and Zeca, who only wanted to play with their catapults and whistles, and that one day soon he'd go to Bairro Operário and get his cousin to take him over to that girl in Sete.

'And what about the money, Zito?'

'Yes, I know, Biquinho. I'll sort it out. Beg, borrow or steal – whatever it takes, I'll find a way.'

And so for weeks and weeks he could think about nothing else, wherever he went. Whenever he got washed and dressed, whenever he saw Carmindinha, whenever he went to bed, there lurking in the dark he could hear his cousin's words.

Yes, it was that hot night that brought all the bad luck. Just thinking about it – which by now is every time he looks at Carmindinha or spies on Toneta from behind the fence in Granny Xica's backyard – makes him ache inside. He wants to cry but he can't; he wants to run far away where he can't hear his cousin's words or the noises coming from the other side of the hut in the heat of the night after the rains and which he now knows are neither the cockroaches nor the rats, as Mama Sessá once told him long ago when he'd asked.

Every time he thinks about that night, Zito wants either to flee far, far away, or stand his ground and conquer Carmindinha

– or maybe even Toneta, who he's never seen properly despite all his creeping around like a chicken thief. That's when he swears he'll get the money, even if he has to steal it, and go to his cousin over in Bairro Operário to become a man.

So on days like these when the incessant drumming of the rain on the roof made your head spin and there was nothing to do but stay indoors, his cousin's words, the noises from the hut, the women crouching down with their legs open under the tamarind tree, everything ran like the rain through Zito's head and the boy could do nothing but stare at Carmindinha, catching a glimpse whenever she raised her arm, watching when she sat down, peering when she climbed up on a chair to put things away. Just like he was doing that very moment.

'Zito, pass me that towel over there!'

From the door of the bedroom, Mrs Domingas pointed at the towel folded on the table. Inside, on the floor, Carmindinha's wet clothes whispered his cousin's words. Zito's blood began to flow and his hands trembled as he handed Mrs Domingas the towel. Outside, Zeca and Xoxombo's gleeful shrieks made him want to go and thump them.

'Come on, hurry up! Are you sick or something, boy? Take that look off your face!'

Sitting on the floor mat as Tunica's expert fingers deftly defeated a distracted Biquinho at pebbles, Zito could just make out through the half-closed door the wet clothes lying on the floor and glimpses of Carmindinha's body being washed by Mrs Domingas: the slim, firm buttocks, the tiny nipples on her chest, her clear, shining skin. Even with the noise of the rain on the tin roof, he could hear the rustle of the dress slipping down over her body.

Outside, with no wind to drive it away, the rain continued to fall thick and hot. The shifting black clouds revealed occasional patches of blue, thunder and lightning shook the trees, and thick streams gnawed their way through the sands between the huts, draining away in great reddish rivers that carried the sand and rubbish of the *musseques* down towards the city.

Mrs Sessá, Zito's mum, swore at the water as it began to seep into her hut. You could hear Albertina's voice, hoarse with drink, singing something rude as she piled all her belongings on top of the table so the stream of dirty water could flow straight through her living room and out into the backyard. Barefoot and almost naked, Albertina splashed around heavily, helping the rainwater on its way with her feet. Walls turned darker as they got wet and bits of mud started to flake off. Many people had already come out with barrel hoops and machetes to try to divert the water away from their huts, but the water flowed on regardless straight through Granny Xica's front door, filling the rooms, soaking her floor mats and leaving an indelible stain of red mud. Granny Xica, who was more than seventy years old according to Captain Bento, stood in her doorway and, raising her feeble arms and clapping her hands, shouted with all the force that remained in her frail old body.

'*Aiuê*! My poor house! Help! Help!'

Playing down below in the great puddle where all the little rivers joined together before gushing on down towards Rua da Pedreira, Zeca and Xoxombo heard the old woman's shouts and came running. Xoxombo dashed through into her backyard, grabbed the barrel hoop and took command of the situation.

'Come on, Zeca! Start making a mud wall in the doorway! Quick!'

Still clapping her hands, Granny Xica watched the boys as the rain beat down on their naked backs and their little hands scraped together a wall of mud from beneath the waters. Zeca and Xoxombo were delighted that no one else came to help – for once, there were no grown-ups to tell them off, and they were the ones saving Granny Xica and all her belongings from being swept away by the floods. Their little mud wall held and the angry, red-foamed water ran down the little channel Xoxombo had cut along the wall, leading it away in the direction of the bakery where it joined with the great torrent cascading down towards Ingombota.

By the time Mrs Domingas appeared with Zito, both of them soaked through and with the rain still falling, the water had stopped coming into the old woman's house. Angry at the boys, Mrs Domingas splashed straight through Xoxombo's channel. The boys stood up proudly, looked at the two women and Zito, and congratulated themselves.

'*Pópilas*, Zeca!' exclaimed Xoxombo. 'Just look what I did – skilful or what?'

'Don't talk rubbish! If it wasn't for me building the wall, the whole hut would've been washed away!'

'Yeah, well, but I'm the one who made the water go away. Look – see what I mean?'

Mrs Domingas helped lift things off the floor. Everything was soaked and dirty – the baskets of flour had turned to a thick, reddish, mushy pap and the mat was stuck to the floor with the mud.

'*Aiuê*! All ruined!' wailed Granny Xica. 'What's to become of me? What's the use of me having a granddaughter, then?'

'Don't worry, grandma,' said Mrs Domingas. 'I'm here to help. And Toneta – isn't she at work?'

'Her? At work? Gracious no! She isn't even out of bed yet!'

'What? And that man of hers?'

'He's gone off to Caxito, my dear,' said Granny Xica, shaking her head. 'So she decided she'd skip work.'

Mrs Domingas managed to lift the mat off the floor and began rolling it up.

'Zito!' she called out. 'Come here and take this mat out to the backyard where the rain'll wash it.'

The poor boy was soaked through. His white shirt was stuck to his skin and his shorts were dripping down his thick thighs, but even then he wouldn't hear of staying to play with Xoxombo and Zeca in the rain. He only wanted to hear what Granny Xica had to say about Toneta. When he'd heard she was still in bed, he could once again feel his blood pumping, the desire both to run away and to stay, thinking that this might be the moment Toneta would call him over. So he quickly washed the mat, his heart beating and his eyes fixed on the open window, the window where he'd so often peeked in hoping to see Toneta getting undressed. He leaned the mat against the cassava bush and came back inside the hut. Toneta was standing in the middle of the room, watching her grandmother and Mrs Domingas sweep away the water with an old yard brush made of palm leaves.

She was wearing only a slip over her gleaming black skin – the skin which all the women in the *musseque* envied and all the men desired. The almost imperceptible movement of the fabric was enough to reveal the outline of her jutting thighs. Zito, standing in the doorway, couldn't stop staring at her firm buttocks, the ones he'd so often glimpsed when Toneta headed off to work every morning, hips swaying.

'For Christ's sake, woman!' yelled Toneta. 'I'm the one who earns the money – can't I get some sleep? Who buys the food around here? Well? And who pays the rent?'

Granny Xica couldn't bring herself to answer, and Mrs Domingas shook the brush at her angrily. Toneta picked her way across the red mud. The sound of her footsteps woke Zito from his reverie and the lad's gaze swept from her ankles up those strong, firm legs. His cousin's words screamed in his ears so loudly he could almost see them. But this wasn't some girl from Sete he'd never even met. This was Toneta, Granny Xica's granddaughter, the scarlet woman of our *musseque* who was sleeping with that Mr Amaral, some sort of lowly clerk at the Department of Agriculture with his skinny legs, crooked back and hacking cough.

Aiuê! How many times during those long, hot nights had Zito raged inside, wanting to go and knock down that door and punch Mr Amaral's pasty white face? Lying there coughing in Toneta's bed, beside those firm buttocks he'd spied on so many times from the *mulemba* tree? The rain was still drumming on the tin roof above his head but he couldn't hear it, nor Mrs Domingas calling him angrily as she put down the brush.

'Shoo, Zito! Go home, boy. Go back to your mother – I'm sure she needs you.'

Zito watched Toneta's body silhouetted against the light pouring in through the front door, filling the hut with the sound of the rain and of Zeca and Xoxombo playing in the pools of muddy water outside. He watched her beautiful, full breasts rise and fall as she turned angrily to the two women, cursing and threatening them. Mrs Domingas quickly grabbed the boy to pull him out of the hut before he heard any more swearing, but Toneta wasn't having any of it.

'Leave the kid alone! No one's going to eat him!'

Her hot hand, still full of sleep and bed, ran down his wet back and skilfully pulled him back inside the hut.

'Shameless hussy! yelled Mrs Domingas, banging on the door. 'You and your filthy thoughts – and him only a boy!'

Granny Xica went out into the yard, shaking her head and muttering.

The rain had gone, leaving just a few black clouds in the sky. Pretty patches of blue were starting to appear and a yellow sun was trying to break through. Standing in front of Toneta, Zito trembled.

'Aw, poor thing! Look at you standing there, all dripping wet!'

He'd been waiting for this moment for so long. Zito tried to speak, tried to say all those things his cousin had told him grown men say. It wounded him the way Toneta was speaking to him like he was Zeca or Xoxombo, but still the words stuck in his throat.

'Come on then! I'll clean you up. Hurry up – don't look at me like that!'

Toneta saw the lad's eyes staring at her breasts. They seemed to be trying to escape from under her loose slip.

'What's this? Never seen a woman before?' Toneta laughed. 'Come on, then!'

His feet wouldn't move, but her warm hands propelled him towards the bedroom. As they entered, Zito felt an overwhelming desire to turn and grab the girl, but his courage failed him. Frozen like a statue, he let Toneta's warm hands pull off his shirt, his heart pounding.

'*Aiuê*, you poor little thing! Just look! You'll catch your death of cold, soaked to the skin like that!'

But Zito couldn't hear Toneta's words. He could only sense the softness of her voice, her shining white teeth, her warm laugh in the darkness of the room. The rumpled sheets on the big bed revealed the hollow in the middle that still smelt of Toneta's warm body, still held the outline of her smooth buttocks, her wide hips and her long, firm legs. But Mr Amaral was also there – an empty cup on the bedside table, two little flasks of cough medicine, a pair of trousers hanging on the end of the bed.

His blood welled up with anger at the old man, a deep pain that made him lean on Toneta, kneeling in front of him drying his legs. The boy's strong fingers dug into the soft skin of Toneta's rounded shoulders.

'Hey there, kid! Be careful – that hurts!'

Lifting those big, still eyes of hers, Toneta laughed, her charcoal-whitened teeth gleaming, as she rubbed the boy's chest, back and arms, laughing, stroking and murmuring in his ear.

'Fine, strong lad! So what's your name, then?'

'Zito. José Domingos, that is…'

Still laughing, she stood up slowly, making sure he got a good look at her smooth, black, gleaming breasts and the darkness beyond.

'Take off your shorts so I can wash you.'

Zito looked into Toneta's eyes, startled. Her voice was soft and kind and warm and he liked it when she said 'fine, strong lad'. But suddenly now, even smiling that same smile, almost naked in front of him, it sounded like his mum's voice telling him off when he came home dirty from playing in the street. Seeing the shame in his eyes, Toneta stopped laughing and, holding his arms, brought her face close to his.

'I know. You're a man now. That's it, isn't it Zito? You don't just take off your shorts like that any more.'

Zito pulled her towards him and Toneta crumpled against his chest. He felt her soft breasts against his body and his blood pounded in his ears.

'Hey! What's this? Now don't get angry with me, Zito! When I want I can be a good girl and when I want I can be a bad girl…'

Her laugh, her words and the words of his cousin

somersaulted around inside him. He touched Toneta's face and tried hard to say all the words his cousin had taught him, but his head was spinning. He could feel his blood boiling; he could see her breasts swaying slowly back and forth, the bed over there behind them, Mr Amaral's empty cup and medicine bottles. The tears that had been welling up inside him came rushing out, down his chest, his hands, Toneta's face.

'I really like you...' he spluttered.

Not even Zeca and Xoxombo's shouts, or Mama Sessá (who'd got wind from Mrs Domingas what that shameless hussy was up to with her son) calling from the doorway of the hut, could stop him. Running shirtless through the rivers of red water his black legs splattered with mud, he disappeared up towards the tamarind tree. It wasn't for another two hours that Mama Sessá and Mrs Domingas finally got their hands on him and with a branch from the *mulemba* tree gave him the fiercest beating he'd ever had.

All the others kids watched from a safe distance, just so they could console him afterwards, of course. They were all surprised when Zito reappeared and, with that grown-up air of his, merely smiled at them.

'*Pópilas!*' he exclaimed through his tears. 'I needed a good thrashing!'

2

'Xoxombo, you remember that day with the St Anthony?'

'Come on, Zito! How could I forget it?'

It had been carnival time. All the *musseque* kids had made masks out of cardboard and were chucking handfuls of flour at each other. They chased and fought, shrieking with laughter until some idiot went too far and punched someone in the eye.

Toneta was standing in the door of her hut – back then she wasn't yet sleeping with Mr Amaral – and the boys stopped their messing around to stare at her, dressed up like Carmen Miranda in all her film star glory.

'*Pópilas*, Zito! You remember Zeca's face? Like he was crazy, he was grinning so much!'

'I'll never forget it, swear to God!'

Toneta called the boys over. Zeca Bunéu and Xoxombo went over right away but Biquinho rushed off to get Zito, Carmindinha and Tunica, telling them that Granny Xica's granddaughter was going to show them some sort of magic trick. Mrs Domingas muttered something under her breath about shameless something-or-other, but the four of them went over anyway to see what she had to show them. It was a little St Anthony made out of wood, dressed in a piece of brown cloth tied with a cord around his waist. He had purple eyes, drawn on with colouring pencil and spit. Toneta picked up the doll and they all sat down on the mat.

'Everyone close their eyes,' she ordered, 'and think of what you want St Anthony to give you. But don't say it out loud.'

They all did as they were told, asking St Anthony inside their heads for whatever it was they wanted.

'Right, okay. Now you can look.'

Kneeling in front of them, Toneta held St Anthony by the cord around his waist and put on a very serious face. But Zito, without meaning to, caught a look in her eyes and saw she was up to something. There was a piece of string hanging down from the doll's feet. Toneta looked around their solemn little faces, their curious eyes all fixed on St Anthony, and made her choice.

'You!' she said, pointing at Zito. 'Have you chosen what you want?'

Zito nodded.

'Well, then, pull this string and out it'll come!'

The other kids looked at the lucky friend who was going to get his present first, and started whispering amongst themselves.

'Ssssh!' hissed Toneta. 'It won't work if you make a noise.'

Zito warily stretched out his hand, saw the mischief gleaming in Toneta's eyes and started to laugh.

'*Pópilas*! I asked for a bike!' he blurted out, and yanked the string.

What happened next is almost painful to tell. Toneta and Zeca Bunéu, always the rascal, roared with laughter. Carmindinha's face, serious and angry, mirrored Zito's. He'd been tricked. Tunica sobbed quietly. Toneta let go of the St Anthony and it fell onto the mat, the big fat cock with its reddened head still poking out through the brown fabric from when Zito pulled the string.

'Bloody hell, Zito – she certainly got the better of you, didn't she!'

'Well, I'll never forget that day,' Zito replied ruefully.

It was this conversation about the St Anthony that led to all the trouble. Zito needed someone to talk to and, even though Xoxombo was only little, it was to him that Zito went to talk over all the morning's nonsense, and how he was really worried now about spying on Toneta. What would he do if she called him into her room?

Xoxombo was still a little boy, but he had sisters.

'I don't know, Zito. But if I were you,' he advised solemnly, 'I'd get her a present and take it over to her next time you go.'

By now it was a sultry mid-afternoon. When the heavy rains come, the wet sands breathe out all the water as soon as the fierce yellow sun appears in the cloudless blue sky. Even with the freshness of the rains, people were beginning to feel the windless heat that brings warm, sticky nights – nights when you sit chatting on the doorstep until late and then sleep with all the windows open. Swallows swooped through the freshly washed air and sparrows twittered from the tin roofs. Lush green grass sprouted everywhere and the *muxixi* and baobab trees, their roots full of water, seemed to be laughing at the sun.

As they headed down into the city, ducking and diving to make sure Mrs Domingas didn't see them and then racing down Rua da Pedreira, Xoxombo really saw that Zito was nearly grown-up, just like everyone else was saying. It was almost half past five and he was a young man in a hurry. Xoxombo was scared stiff and kept looking all around him as they walked through Ingombota, worried there might be friends of his mother's who'd tell on him. He was already wishing he hadn't said anything to Zito. *Pópilas*! Why did he always want to do everything straight away? And how on earth had he managed to get his hands on that twenty *angolar* note?

With all of these thoughts racing around his head and his little heart full of fear, Xoxombo scarcely even noticed that they'd arrived downtown. The streets and houses were pretty – no tin-roofed huts here, that's for sure, and the roads were full of cars and people, and neatly tarred, unlike all that sand in the *musseques*. Zito walked fearlessly through the streets as if he owned them, not even bothering to get out of the way of the cars. Nothing flummoxed him. But Xoxombo was afraid, and he couldn't stop thinking that this very minute Mrs Domingas would be standing in the doorway of her hut, calling for him in that way of hers so familiar to everyone in the *musseque*,

'Xoxombo! Xoxomboaaay!'

When he didn't appear, Mrs Domingas would go back inside to get her wooden spoon ready for when he reappeared.

Maybe she'd already gone over to Mama Sessá's and told the rest of the neighbours about them running off. And then there was the money – how on earth had Zito got his hands on twenty *angolares*? As he mulled it over, he scarcely noticed his friend's chirpiness, wrapping and unwrapping the earrings – little yellow flowers made of tin. His feet carried him faster and faster now, back up through the throngs of people in Ingombota heading home from work. He'd been gone all afternoon and by now they'd be looking for him all over the *musseque*. Zito whistled contentedly – he kept putting the little package in his pocket, then taking it out and unwrapping it and admiring the little yellow flowers.

'Oh for goodness' sake, Xoxombo! Why are you still such a baby?'

Xoxombo didn't reply. Right now, that was exactly what he wanted – to be so small, so tiny, that he could sneak into the house without anyone seeing him and snuggle up on the mattress. Then, when it was seven or eight o'clock and mum started shouting for him, he could appear from the bedroom pretending he'd spent the whole afternoon in there sleeping because he was so tired from playing all morning in the rain. But how was he going to get into the house like that, without anyone seeing him?

Everything was quiet in the *musseque*. The only sounds that greeted them were hens clucking over their chicks, birds singing from the trees and muffled voices from inside the huts. The sun, red as the sand, muddied the sky's deep blue as it sank towards the sea.

'Thanks, Xoxombo. You're a real mate. I'm off home now.'

'Already? And what'll I say if they ask me?'

'Dunno – up to you. But don't say anything about the earrings or what we talked about. Here, keep this. If we can get away on Saturday, I'll take you to the matinée at the National.'

Xoxombo stood staring at the coin in his hand, and watched Zito move with the stealth of a leopard up towards the tamarind tree. As usual, he'd be hiding until it was dark and he could peer at Toneta in Granny Xica's backyard. Putting the coin in his pocket, Xoxombo jumped over the fence, crept across the yard and climbed up into the *mulemba* tree. As his fears subsided he started to whistle. Mrs Domingas wasn't there – she'd gone over to Granny Xica's and it was Carmindinha's face that appeared beneath the tree.

'Xoxombo, have you seen Tunica?' she asked.

He carried on whistling like a grown-up, not paying the slightest attention to his sister down below. Then, feeling rather cheeky and full of himself, replied, 'Up your bum!'

Carmindinha told him to grow up and went back inside.

3

So when was it then? How did it start? Why couldn't she get that kid out of her head, out of her hands? The whole afternoon, hot already, window and door shut, birds outside, sun seeping in, granny's slow footsteps in the house, in the backyard, talking to herself, people laughing in the street. Tossing and turning in bed, getting up, sitting down, getting dressed, getting undressed. And what was the story with the medicine bottles? Why all the shards of glass in the corner and a dark stain on the floor?

'I really like you...'

Once before, a long time ago, there'd been another fine, strong lad. Time and again she waited for him, slept with him, and then he left. How come? When? Before Mr Amaral, long before then. Hard to remember. Now just the old man's coughing, that medicine smell from his yellow body, those shrieks like an old woman's and that buffalo breathing of his that scared her, made her think he was going to die or something.

'So then, my little Toneta? I'm asking you, and I don't like asking...' he laughs, and she can see his fetid mouth, his tobacco-stained teeth.

It's been ages since she slept with a man.

But think of the dresses you'd like, the shoes, money to pay the rent, money to buy food, Granny Xica always complaining about Mr Antunes's prices. And for all that: come here Toneta, sit down Toneta, stand up Toneta, lie down Toneta. Yuck! And the yuckiest thing of all, that time at work with the boss down at the telephone exchange making fun of her.

'Hey there, Toneta! You just let me know when you bump the old man off. I'll be there. At the cemetery, of course,' he winked.

And Zito?

That fine lad who came in out of the rain, that strong lad who wouldn't let her take off his shorts, shaking with embarrassment but bold enough to spy on her every afternoon, sobbing bravely.

'I really like you...'

He said his name was Zito. It would be good taking him to bed, bury his head in her flesh as his tears came flooding out, run her fingers down his back, his strong arms, his firm stomach. Like a big baby, but a man.

The body moves, the bed squeaks. She covers her ears, not wanting to let the noise spoil the image in her head. A fine, strong lad, his eyes fixed hungrily on her faded, pink slip, almost naked...

She gets out of bed and opens the window, barefoot. The

fresh smell of damp earth floods in, the six o'clock sun setting behind the Balão tower, the leaves on the cassava bush rustling in the backyard, the birds singing their evening chorus. She peers out and scans the fence trying to spot those chicken thief leopard eyes, but there is nothing, no one. Just Granny Xica dozing on a mat under the cassava bush, her old tobacco pipe lying in the basket of beans she'd started picking earlier that afternoon.

So why isn't he coming today? But then, why would he come, Toneta? You, Zito, you just don't understand, you don't know anything about life, this rotten mess of a life. You fall into the muddy river and even if you can swim there's a crocodile that pulls you away from the bank. But it doesn't kill you there and then, oh no. It pulls you down, down until you're trapped in the mud and die, slowly. That's why the strong lad, the boy with the wet shorts, ran off.

'Zito, isn't that what he said his name was? I bet you he was there that day with the St Anthony!'

She comes back to the window but says nothing. Granny might wake up and then if the boy turned up…

The sun played in the leaves of the cassava bush and then, as it dipped, glowed red on Granny Xica's wrinkled face, driving away the afternoon flies and leaving her to doze peacefully, her beans spilling over the mat.

Oh, come on, Toneta – use your head! You're grown-up now and you like Zito. At work they're always groping you, pulling you in – men treat you like dirt, Toneta, and you do the same to them. There's no point trying to forget those foul-mouthed, tobacco-stained words of the old white man with his disgusting cough. Just think about it, Toneta! How come your heart's pounding for everyone to see, even beneath your slip, just because somewhere down there in the long grass a shy, fearful, barefoot boy is edging slowly towards you, trying to duck the last rays of evening sun? For goodness' sake, Toneta, you're too old to tremble like this – you're not some blushing virgin any more!

The window's open and Granny Xica's fast sleep. What are you waiting for, Zito? Framed by the window, Toneta appears as a bright flash of laughter against the dark outlines of the bedroom. His eyes stare at the hand beckoning him in, his bare feet turn to leopard's paws and he creeps past Granny Xica, leaving her to her dreams in the shade of the cassava bush. Toneta laughs when she opens the door, and it's the same laugh as the morning. His blood rushes through him at the touch of her warm, soft hands.

'Fine, strong lad…' she murmurs.

She turns to shut out the last reds and blues of the sky still peeping through the window, and as she walks, barefoot, her firm buttocks dance beneath her slip and her breasts strain against the straps. When Toneta turns back, Zito closes his eyes.

There's none of his crying from the morning, none of her laughing from washing him after the rain. They just hold each other tight and the heat of his blood, his cousin's words and Toneta's soft murmurings all rush together, pulling off his shirt, his shorts, then the sheets, a shaft of sunlight from a crack in the shutters, blue and red sky, their shining, sweating bodies, still, firm, fine lad, strong lad, naughty boy, badly brought-up *musseque* boy, and Toneta the slut, Mr Amaral's floozy, the ire of all the women and the delight of all the men in our *musseque*.

'So tell me then, Toneta, do you really like me?'

'Yes, Zito, I like you a lot. You're a man.'

Zito laughs, unsure.

'Really?'

Toneta doesn't reply. Silence, air and time slip by.

'Do you know something, Zito? It's been ages since I slept with a man.'

'What about Mr Amaral, then?'

'Mr Amaral?'

The question comes as an echo or a vague memory. Mr Amaral – hasn't he gone to Caxito? Something to do with work?

'Mr Amaral isn't a man.'

'Why? Just because he's old?'

'It's not that, Zito. You won't understand.'

Toneta's hands on his sweating head and resting muscles are like Mama Sessá's when he was a little boy. But now you're a man, Zito, firm and strong and hard like a *mulemba* stick – you're not Mama Sessá's little boy any more.

'Toneta, do you think it's wrong to say rude things?'

'Like what?'

His voice is different, from far away – the other Zito's, the one she doesn't know.

'I don't know, Zito. But if the grown-ups say them…'

'That's what I mean.'

Her hand strokes his ear, touches his head lying against her breast, and stretches out against his still, motionless body.

'Do you really like me, Toneta?'

'Why?'

Zito doesn't know what to say. He can't think of the right words. Best thing would be to give her the present. But the words come anyway.

'Toneta, if you really like me, does that mean you'd never beat me?'

'Never, Zito. Never. For goodness' sake, Zito. No way!'

Why's he saying things like this?

'Are you leaving, Zito?'

'What? No! I'll never leave!'

Toneta laughs. Good lad.

'Zito, does Mama Sessá beat you a lot?'

'Please, Toneta. Let's not talk about things like that.'

Toneta watches him reaching for his shirt pocket. He holds out a small, crumpled package.

'Toneta, you remember the St Anthony?'

She nods.

'Well then, close your eyes.'

She laughs loudly, kisses him and obeys. Eyes tight shut, she can hear the sound of fumbling hands unwrapping the crêpe wrapping paper.

'Now you can open them!'

In the palm of his hand, resting on her still breast, are two little yellow flowers the colour of sunshine. Earrings. Her heart beats faster and she has such a lump in her throat she can't speak. Now come on, Toneta – you're not a little girl any more, you're a grown woman. Are you really going to let all these tears run down your face like this morning's rain? Has it been so long since you cried?

'Fine, strong lad.'

Gradually, her warm, soft hands, the heat of the night and the odour of their sweating bodies blot out those cheery little yellow flowers. He lets sleep sooth his cooling blood, his heart beating slowly beneath Toneta's hand.

And so Zito, the bad boy of the *musseque*, drifts softly to sleep as if cradled in his mother's arms, while Toneta releases the clean, clear water she's been keeping for so long in the deep well of her life, and lies there gazing at the little yellow flowers on his chest.

'My little boy. My fine, strong boy.'

4

It's already half past eight and all the stars are shining on Granny Xica, still sleeping under the cassava bush. Toneta has stopped crying and just stays there, quite still, watching the boy's chest rise and fall as he sleeps. A hot, sticky calm runs through the *musseque*, no wind in the streets, no moon in the sky, just some crazy stars falling out of the sky from time to time. Palm oil and paraffin lamps glimmer in the darkness and a soft silence descends in the heat of the sultry night, not even a breath of air to rattle the tin roofs.

Suddenly the silence fills with voices, shouts, children crying, running footsteps and words that in the darkness seem even louder, more threatening. Angry hands beat on the door, echoing through the hut. Toneta wakes up. Granny Xica, startled, rises slowly from her mat.

'*Aiuê*, go away!' she calls out in her old, worn-out voice. 'Oh, all right then – hold on!'

But whoever's at the door is angry and can't wait. There's a faint sobbing and the sound of furious women. Granny Xica shuffles over towards the door but Toneta races past her and flings it open.

'For Christ's sake!' she shouts out into the night. 'What sort of way is that to knock? Clear off!'

'Out of my way, you little trollop! I'm so angry I'll slap your face, you shameless bitch!'

Mama Sessá emerges from the night into the flickering yellow lamplight, her hands raised. 'Tart! Thief!' she shouts. 'Where's my money?'

In a flash, Toneta grabs her sleeve and pulls her inside, lashing out in rage at the insults. Zito's mother, skinny and

112

strong, kicks and spits in her face, pulls her hair and in an instant the two women are rolling around on the floor, knocking against the table and overturning the wicker baskets. Granny Xica runs out into the street with the lamp as the two of them scratch, swear and pull at each other.

'Vampire! Witch!' screams Toneta.

'The only witch is the mother who gave birth to you, you little whore!' retorts the other.

Sebastião Mateus, Zito's dad, comes running, calling over to Zeca who was in the middle of a conversation with his friends at the grocery store.

'It's a shameful business, brother 'Bastião!' declares Mrs Domingas as she collides with him on his way. 'Now that witch is even fighting with Sessá!'

The news ran quickly through the whole *musseque* that Mama Sessá was trying to kill Toneta. In less than a minute Don'Ana, Dona Branca and Albertina were also standing at the door of the hut watching the two women writhe around on the floor, screaming and swearing at each other. Zeca's dad, still pulling on his trousers, was right behind them, just in time to catch sight of Toneta's legs flailing in the air as she grabbed the older woman by the hair.

'*Aiuê*! Good Lord above! Did you ever see the like? Hurry, man. You too, brother 'Bastião. Help me separate them.'

Zito's dad, a quietly spoken stonemason, had just arrived at the scene, and he didn't like women's arguments.

'Just leave them to it, sister Domingas. Sessá can handle her.'

By now, Zito's mum was indeed on top of Toneta, clawing at her face.

'*Aiuê*! Help! She's going to kill me!'

'Take that! And that! And that! Shameless witch! Slut!'

No one was keen to intervene in their quarrel – better to let the women work off their anger. By now, Granny Xica was outside with her lamp, and the yellow faces of everyone standing round the doorway watching the fight looked like something from a film.

'Sweet Jesus! God help us!' cried out Dona Branca. 'That wretched woman's going to kill the girl!'

'Good for her! The little slut! Her and her filthy ways, messing around with the boys. So what are you laughing at, then?'

Carmindinha stifled her laugh. Her mother's angry face was not to be argued with. She took Tunica off to comfort Xoxombo, who was standing over against the wall. Zeca was there too, craftily trying to get a good look at Toneta's tits and legs in the flurry of fighting. Xoxombo was bawling his eyes out.

'It's not your fault, Xoxombo. Zito's gone crazy or something. You did the right thing. What else could you do?'

'No, Zeca,' he sobbed angrily, biting his hands. 'Zito told me not to tell, and I told.'

It wasn't the bruises all over his body from the wooden spoon – at times like this you don't feel the pain. But how was he going to look Zito in the eye – Zito who had promised to take him to the cinema? What was he going to say now that he'd told?

'Come on, Xoxombo – let's go.' It was Carmindinha's voice beside him, bending down, taking his hand and wiping his snotty nose. 'If they hadn't beaten you, Xoxombo, you wouldn't have told. Zito knows that.'

Zeca nodded in agreement. 'Everyone knows you're not a coward, Xoxombo. Everyone knows you don't tell tales. But they gave you such a beating, for goodness' sake! Even Zito would have squealed.'

Sitting on the sand, Tunica was crying too, feeling her brother's pain. The fighting inside was still going on – it seemed like it was never going to end. Sebastião Mateus had finally gone in to separate them and grabbed his wife's arms. She was trying to break free, spitting at Toneta and hurling every insult she could think of. In the corner of the room Toneta was trying to shield herself with her torn slip from the stares of Zeca's dad, while Granny Xica just shook her head and wept.

'Where's the money, you bitch? Whore!'

At that word, Toneta flung herself once again at Mama Sessá, but Dona Branca got in there in time to hold her back.

'Toneta, you better just say where it is.'

'She can bloody well find it herself!' she shouted furiously. 'Isn't he her own son, from her own womb? I don't keep infants here!' her hand pointing between her legs.

Zito's mother carried on with her insults, calling her a thief and recounting the whole story to Sebastião, although he still couldn't really figure out what was going on. He thought the fuss was all just about Zito sleeping with Toneta and on that score, deep down, he was rather pleased. Yes sir – his own son had got the better of all those other men in the *musseque* trying to get into that girl's bed! But, in the midst of all the tears and swearing, Mama Sessá told him about the twenty *angolares* Zito had taken, the twenty *angolares* she'd been saving up to buy material to make a dress. And this little piece of filth, this witch, had stolen the money off him in return for sleeping with him. Sebastião Domingos Mateus, a serious man, stood there staring at the girl crouching in the corner. Then, with his customary calm, he pushed his wife out through the door and handed her over to Mrs Domingas to take care of. Then he went back into the hut, walked over to Toneta and slapped her twice in the face. Everyone stopped talking. Xoxombo's distant sobbing drifted over on the light breeze, making the flame of the lamp tremble.

'Where's the money?'

Toneta started to cry. It wasn't her stinging cheeks that hurt, but Mr Sebastião's words. She'd always said he was a good man, the only one in the whole *musseque* who didn't look at her with those greedy eyes.

'Cross my heart, brother 'Bastião! I never saw the money.'

She carried on crying, great shaking sobs. She no longer had the strength to hold up her torn slip, even if Zeca's dad was still staring over at her. Her fingers reached towards her ears for the little yellow flowers, the earrings Zito had given her. Sebastião Mateus strode across the room and flung open the bedroom door. Toneta ran and grabbed him, crying.

'*Aiuê,* brother! Don't blame him,' she begged him. 'Swear to God, it's all my fault. I promise!'

Zito, sullen-faced and head hanging, was pulled into the room like some sort of puppet, tripping over the baskets and banging into the table. His father's rough, stonemason hands pounded him all over while Toneta struggled to protect the boy she liked so much, but there wasn't much she could do.

Seeing Toneta clinging to Sebastião as he lashed out at Zito, Mama Sessá came running back in to protect her husband from the girl's anger. That's where Zeca's dad came to her rescue, seizing the opportunity to grope Toneta as he pushed her into the bedroom.

'Hold it, girl!' he whispered softly. 'Save your strength for other things…'

Toneta stayed in the bedroom, venting her anger in screams and curses. Mrs Domingas congratulated Mama Sessá.

'Quite right, sister,' she said smugly. 'It's hussies like her who're corrupting our young men!'

Ignoring them completely, angry at everything and everyone, Mr Sebastião gripped Zito by the arm. As the boy twisted and turned like a goat in the stonemason's grasp, he pulled his son outside and told him he was going to teach him a lesson never to steal money. Tripping and stumbling, Zito somehow managed to find the strength to escape his father's tight grip. He ran over to the wall where Xoxombo, consoled by his friends, had finally stopped crying, and spat at the little boy.

'Fucking tell-tale idiot!' he shouted, seething with anger.

As the hot, starry night descended, people from all over the *musseque* could hear the sound of the stick hitting Zito's body, over and over. What they didn't hear was Zito crying. And when silence returned to the *musseque*, Xoxombo, still sobbing in the doorway of his hut, his heart bursting with shame and happiness, said,

'That Zito is a man!'

There was nothing Carmindinha, Tunica or Zeca Bunéu could say to that.

VI

This is what really happened and I'm not ashamed to say because back then Zito had just come out of jail and I liked him, or felt sorry for him, I'm not sure which. Since I was already going to my sewing, he'd come and wait for us every afternoon on the Calçada da Missão, buy us pastries and Joanica and Tereza would burst out laughing at all the silly things he'd say, but not me.

I didn't laugh but I wanted to and so I just laughed to myself inside, because I was scared of Zito. I couldn't bring myself to trust him ever since that time with Toneta so I kept my mouth shut. Or maybe I was angry about her, but even today I don't really know, and if I'm not sure I suppose it's better to say nothing.

I really hated having to tell Joanica and Tereza the whole story when he didn't turn up that afternoon. They were both older than me and talked about things I only half knew about, but still I told them.

Mind you, their answers weren't any help. 'I don't know. Think carefully.' Well I'd already done that. 'You're still a child, be careful.' Well I knew that too, and I also knew I wasn't a child any more, otherwise Zito wouldn't have asked me to meet him, because he already knew lots of girls. I was quite sure of that; actually I'd swear to it.

And the way my friends were being so careful annoyed me. I asked them why should I be careful when he only wanted to talk to me and surely there was no harm in that? Joanica wouldn't answer and I saw her eyes turn sad, but later on I found out that, for her too, it had been 'only want to talk', then her boyfriend had really messed her up and no one had ever heard anything more from him since.

I can't remember what I felt when they told me. The only thing I remember is what mum said to me that night she fought with dad over the sewing school: 'Sukuama! I don't believe it! Maybe there is, but it's a school for sluts!'

I didn't pay any attention to Joanica and Tereza's warnings and decided I'd go anyway. Zito couldn't harm me – we'd known each other since we were kids. I'd no reason to think anything bad about him.

It was a beautiful, cool night when I went out into the yard, and Zito was there waiting for me. How he got there I don't know, even standing right there under the mulemba tree I didn't spot him. None of the hens, or even Espanhola, made a sound. Then I remembered that when he walked he prowled like a leopard, and that made me smile. We sat under the mulemba tree and I shivered. It wasn't really cold, mind you – July was racing by and the chilly nights were almost over, but there was a moon, a full, white moon, and maybe that's what made it feel colder. I remember the moon because Zito kept insisting it looked like an old man carrying all his belongings on his back.

I teased him, told him that was just lies made up by the priest in our catechism classes at the Mission. Then I explained what my dad, the old sailor, had told me. But Zito was still angry and said I was lying and the moon couldn't possibly have hills and forests or else they'd all fall back down to earth.

'So what about the old man, then?'

Zito didn't reply. Well there was nothing he could say, and I thought how smart I was and how the moonlight made everything so beautiful and the hanging roots of the mulemba *tree were glistening with drops of mist. Neither of us wanted to talk.*

'So you want to meet up and then you don't say anything. Is that it?'

He laughed. I was scared his laughter would wake up Espanhola. *The kid goat raised her head but she didn't wake up. But still he didn't say anything, just leant his body against mine and, very slowly, put his arms around me. Joanica and Tereza's warnings flashed through my head and I pulled away, but Zito said he'd leave and I said I didn't want him to go.*

He didn't go. He stayed, said nothing, embraced me again and smiled. I laughed too, my silly girlish laugh, and he started talking about jail, the beatings, the prisoners, the shaved heads and all that. I interrupted from time to time. He wanted so much to be a man, but to me he was still just one of the boys from our musseque.

'So why then, Zito?'

His hands touched my body and already I'd forgotten about Espanhola *or what Joanica and Tereza had said and all I could feel was the mist falling, falling, like spilt moonlight, and the voice of the boy from our* musseque *talking about the cigarettes he wanted, the money he didn't have, the places to take a girlfriend (he said he was sorry about that and he didn't like her any more), how he'd seen Dona Guilhermina's pastry seller's money, nicked it, got in a fight, thumped the guy, smashed up his tray and ended up in jail.*

We talked on into the night. I can't remember what it was

we talked about, or rather I remember there were many things, and whatever they were it didn't matter because the night was beautiful and Zito was strong and he held me expertly in his arms, squeezing slowly like a boa constrictor. I felt then that everything would be fine in the morning after a night like that, I could do whatever I wanted, run barefoot through the dewy grass, feel the cold drops on my skin, watch the birds soar far away, the grasshoppers, the spiders' webs glistening in the early morning sun, or maybe I'd fall into one of Zeca's grass-roped animal traps and just lie there covered in little drops of water laughing, laughing to my heart's content until mum called me to go and fetch some water.

Once again came Zito's deep voice, saying those things that frightened me the day he came out of jail and everyone sat round in the house, listening to him talk. I still didn't want to believe it and I asked him if it was really true, that in jail the boys became the women, and he swore it was true and then I cried.

He carried on talking, about the screams of the younger boys and about the older men paying 'Sugarman', who was in charge of the boys. I just kept on crying, not really sure what the boy-women had to do, and Zito didn't want to explain and when he lifted his hands from my body I felt the chill, the chill of that beautiful misty night on my hot body and I leant closer to Zito.

Once again, he was silent. He put an arm around me and his hand reached under my blouse, reaching for my breasts, still small and hard. It felt good like that, his warm hand, but Joanica and Tereza's words came back to me again.

'Zito!'

'What?'

He said that no, I wasn't a slut and he burst out laughing,

*like a child really, like the boy he still was making fun of all
this grown-up stuff. Or at least that's how it seemed to me. So
I laughed too and his hands trembled and it made my breasts
tickle.*

'Was it Joanica who told you…?'

*He was surprised how angry I was. Actually I surprised even
myself. But I really wanted to know if he'd been 'talking' to her
too, if he'd gone out with her, if he'd put his arms around her,
if he'd fondled her too. But then he said, 'So Carmindinha…'
and I didn't say anything more.*

*I didn't like the sound of the wind shaking the hanging roots
of the* mulemba *tree, and they'd already lost their dewy shine.
A cold, sharp gust of wind reached the chicken coop and raised
a few chirps from the little chicks, and once again I was afraid.*

*'It won't wake them up,' I said to Zito. 'Dad only got back
yesterday.'*

*I could feel the mischief in his eyes, his voice and his arm
around my shoulders, and I didn't like it. His hands searched
once again and found, running up and down and now it was
my blood and Zito's breathing rising together and it made me
happy, and I thought to myself how good it was to want a man
like this and that what men do is good and anyone who says
I'm a whore doesn't know what they're talking about. If you
like it, then go ahead and like it – you're only a whore if you do
things you don't like with people you don't like. Then I heard a
noise and I pushed Zito's hands away.*

*But it wasn't mum or even dad. It was just Xoxombo
thumping Tunica in the back because she'd pulled the blanket
away from him leaving him out in the cold, and even in his
sleep the little boy was hitting his sister's back like it was some
sort of drum.*

I could see Zito's eyes shining like a cat as I walked back towards him. I also thought to myself that, yes, it really was the cool season, what with Xoxombo and Tunica fighting like that and the mist and dew running down the corrugated iron roofs, pinging on the ground like music and even trickling inside the houses. In the morning everything would be damp, and Tunica and I would pretend our breath was smoke. Xoxombo didn't know how to do it so he'd cry.

Then his hot hand grabbed me hard, and this time it took my breath away. He held me tight and my skin felt softer and softer every time he ran his hands over it, hotter and hotter with every caress and I remember saying 'no' but Zito didn't pay any attention and pulled me back under the mulemba *tree and I said 'no' and he said 'let me', and then his hands, his eyes, underneath my dress the fire burning inside me even though it was the cool season; tomorrow Xoxombo and Zeca would be making bonfires and the grey and white smoke would mingle with the grey and white clouds rolling across the dull sky, the shirking sun lolling around up there somewhere with the big, cold, white moon, and the little grey and white* pírula *birds calling incessantly through the rain like they were singing to it.*

'No, Zito!' I cried and he didn't listen, but Espanhola *replied from over in her corner and the hens opened their eyes and began clucking and the cock crowed, probably mistaking the cold white moonlight for the weak morning sun.*

The heat was overwhelming, my whole body was taut and very small and I could hardly feel anything any more except his leopard hands running over my fragile, exposed body and my small breasts, as he whispered softly. And it was the cool season, a fine misty night, no heat, no rains, no flies, my favourite time of year. I didn't care if there were no cashews or mangos or avocados or monkey-oranges because there was the mist, the freshness, grass the colour of toasted almonds, the bonfires and those grey clouds, so low you could almost touch them.

Even so, again I said 'No, Zito', and Espanhola *bleated and the cock crowed, fooled once again, and with Zito's mischievous eyes and mine half-closed that's when we both saw the yellow lamplight seeping out from under the back door filling the misty moonlight and mum and dad coming towards us and there was nothing we could do and I tried to hide behind the* mulemba *tree, the cock was still crowing, the hens taking fright and* Espanhola *leaping around in her corner, dark shadows flickering in the yellow lamplight, the whiteness of the yard under the full moon, and I was scared and so I shouted and shouted.*

The lamp came right in front of my eyes and I saw mum and dad's yellow faces of fear and suffering. My body felt weightless, weightless like I was going to fall over. I shook myself free of Zito's arms around me, but he had already gone.

They beat me. Hard at first, then not so hard. They kept on shouting at me and our neighbours Mrs Sessá and Dona Branca came through the misty night to see the girl who was crying. Tunica and Xoxombo awoke from their sleepy tussle and started to cry about me getting a beating, but I didn't say anything. I just sat there looking at the full white moon looming bigger and bigger overhead. Dad swore he'd seen that scoundrel Zito and he was going to beat the truth out of me. I just cried and I didn't want to tell the truth. All those warnings from mum about Joanica and I didn't want them to know I was crying inside because Zito's eyes had been wide open when his hands made my body feel all small and hard like my breasts, and that's when I'd realised that what he really wanted was just to get his way with me and nothing more. I wept tears of anger, deep inside me.

And when they'd called me a shameless hussy, a bitch, a slut, and the whole musseque *had had a good look at my puffed-up face crying tears both inside and outside, I just kept on saying, 'It's a lie! It's a lie! I only came out to see why* Espanhola *was making all that noise!' while the old captain swore to Mama Sessá that Zito had been out to ruin me that very night, and that I was nothing but a slut like Joanica and Tereza, and then he hit me again, yes he'd been right all along, ever since that business about the sewing, and then Albertina appeared.*

Yes, Albertina.

Everyone fell silent, apart from the sound of me crying. The moon was laughing at me, brighter now, like the watery drops of mist falling on the musseque, *the mist I liked so much, that fine misty night, the* mulemba *tree silent too, its hanging roots weeping their teardrops of moonlight, the hens and the cock silent,* Espanhola *peering around with her red goat-eyes, casting a shadow bigger than her. And that's when Albertina spoke.*

I wanted to cry but I couldn't any more. I just cried inside, clinging on to that woman and to this very day I've tried to be as kind as Albertina. And so on that beautiful misty night with drops of moonlight sparkling on the tin roofs of all the huts, when Albertina spoke and I stopped crying, we all followed her across the street, mum holding her lamp, its yellow light casting devilish shadows on the walls and revealing Albertina's bedroom to the whole musseque, *a tiny little room with white moonlight flooding in through an open window, and there was that scoundrel Zito, lying under the covers like he'd been there all his life, like it was the bed he'd been born in and never left, eating, drinking and growing up between those hot sheets of Albertina's who, as the whole* musseque *could see and has talked about ever since, had slept with him that night. Well that shut mum up, and dad hugged me and said he was sorry and I felt so angry with myself, angry with Zito and angry about the lie, but I kept my tears of rage inside, and on the outside I wept only drops of misty moonlight, the white light of the big bright moon falling on the tin roofs of our* musseque *on a beautiful chilly night, that it was Albertina, our very own professional prostitute.*

*

I've written down this story about Zito exactly how Carmindinha told it to me. And given how much I like the girl, if I tell you what happened it isn't because I'm trying to pretend that it hurts me any less how it ended up, with that fine lie about him being in Albertina's bed that misty night. It's just that I promised to tell the truth about Zito.

VII

It was Don'Ana who told me, because I didn't know. And back then the other boys were still too young – all they remember is the woman screaming and nothing else. Mrs Domingas doesn't tell it the same way. There aren't that many differences, but the old sea captain interrupts to warn us that if we want to get the whole story straight for our newspaper then the best thing is to hear it from him. Mrs Domingas isn't having any of it and cuts him off.

'Huh! You cleared off with Zito to the brick yard, and now you think you know better than the rest of us?'

Captain Bento doesn't answer, just mutters that women say things to provoke you and if you pay any attention it just makes things worse, so you're better off just sitting and reading your paper. Then Don'Ana starts by telling us that it was raining really heavily, with drum rolls in the sky and terrifying lightning. Mrs Domingas, with her usual tact, doesn't want to contradict her old friend and neighbour, so she carries on by saying that the night was dark and full of palm oil lamps twinkling in the *musseque* of the heavens. We ask Mama Sessá, Zito's mum, but she has nothing to add.

'Oh goodness, it's so long ago,' she says, shaking her head.

'I don't remember. Zito would know.'

Zito would indeed know, but Zito had been sent to the work camps in São Tomé. And as we'd promised that our newspaper would only tell the truth (which is why Mr Antunes banned Antoninho from reading it), we wanted to find out and so we kept on asking. Then one day we got our chance. Don'Ana was sitting on her own with Tété on her knees, chatting away like she does, and Zeca and I listened carefully to her telling all those stories about when Albertina arrived in our *musseque*, things that were talked about for months and months and are now almost forgotten.

So today I'm going to tell the story as it's written down in our newspaper, in Zeca Bunéu's tiny round handwriting. The article's by Tonito Kadibengu – I can't remember if that was one of Zeca's names or mine. Maybe it was even Antoninho, because right at the end, when Zeca and I were the only ones left in the *musseque*, he used to come and help out.

1

So this is how the grown-ups of our *musseque* tell the story. They say she was in a really bad way, screaming and thrashing around in the bed. And that everyone came out to watch that night she arrived on the arm of the tall man in a white suit, the one they'd already spotted three days earlier. First of all he'd had a good look around the hut and then stood in front with Mr Aníbal Manco, the rent collector, staring at it but not talking to anyone. Our mothers didn't like him, the rent man that is. He walked with a limp and never missed the end of the month – if you didn't have the rent money then he'd come barging right in and start picking out your best stuff. He said the man was from Malanje and was going to live here.

130

Mrs Domingas and Don'Ana, along with Mama Sessá and even Dona Branca, had a lot to say about it during those three days: a white man, well dressed liked that, living here in the *musseque*? Even if the hut had a brand new tin roof and, best of all, a concrete floor (not to mention that there wasn't a single termite, as Mr Aníbal proudly demonstrated by scraping the wall with a barrel hoop). But even so. Well, it would only end in trouble, they tutted.

Don'Ana, who'd only just been widowed, kept saying over and over that the hut was bound to be for someone's little friend – some girl ruined by one of those *ngueta* whites down in the city and set up with a little house, rent and food all paid for, so he could come sneaking up here in the heat of the night like a hyena. Then he'd discover his little poppet's boyfriend between the sheets and that's when the real fun and games would begin, she chortled.

But there was one thing nobody had thought of: the woman was white, and no spring chicken either. They arrived sometime after eight o'clock in the evening, and all the women were sitting chatting on their front steps with their children when suddenly screams and shouts added to the mystery.

'Well I never! No sooner arrived and she's already in the harness!'

'No, sister – can't you hear? Sounds like the poor woman isn't well.'

But all they could hear were the man's footsteps going in and out of the backyard, pots and pans banging, cries of pain.

Captain Abano says it was the man himself who came for help, but you know what people are like in our *musseque* – as soon as anyone hears any shouts or noises or arguments, over they all go, first the women with the kids clutching their skirts, then the men making some kind of excuse and, if it's an illness, asking if they can fetch anything, or slinking off again if it's an argument.

They found the woman twisting and turning in bed, moaning and thrashing around in her nightie, soaked through with sweat. Don'Ana quickly changed it for a dry one she pulled out of a big suitcase in the corner of the room, while Mrs Domingas lit the little iron stove in the backyard. I think that's when the captain shooed out the kids to go and play – he wouldn't even let Carmindinha stay. Then he stood talking to the man in the white suit about the misfortunes of life, these bush fevers that just grab you and before you know it you're dead, and other stuff like that, half telling him and half trying to find out.

In our *musseque*, when you help someone, you want to know why. Even if you're just doing what has to be done. And if it isn't someone like us, you want to know who it is you're helping. Anyway, I'm sticking to the story, even if Mrs Domingas always says her husband didn't see much because he went running off with Zito to pinch a nice new brick from where they were building the high school, and the captain's the only one who talks about those things the women never say and which he swears the man told him that night.

For example: the story that the woman had come from Golungo, daughter of a retired soldier who'd left her lots of shops in little tiny villages out there in the middle of the bush. People would come in to sell wax, coffee, honey and other things, and buy their fabric, beads, liquor and salt – business was brisk in the shops of the white man Mukuangombe, which was what they called him. And he had many, many cattle, nobody knew how many, and children too – white kids and mulatto kids scattered all round the countryside. Every mother's son knew him. And there were other stories that were more difficult to believe.

Don'Ana went even further, swearing that in her fever the woman kept calling for all her children in Malanje – indeed that she'd babbled on about nothing else. 'I swear, sister! That poor woman's suffering from not having those children here with her,' she affirmed two days later, trying to make up excuses why the white woman's door was now firmly closed.

Others weren't so sure, saying it was just the sheer ingratitude of those jumped-up whites, 'If it hadn't been for us she'd be dead there and then – and now just look at her slamming her door in everyone's face!'

It's difficult to know where the truth really lies. It had been a long, hot night with so much going on, and everything happened so quickly like it'd been done that way just to cause confusion. Mama Sessá kept on changing the bedclothes, and the poor woman seemed to be melting in sweat as she lay dozing and waking.

'*Aiuê*!' she moaned. 'My belly! My back! I'm dying!'

She didn't calm down until well after midnight, when her breathing became more regular, her moaning softer and she stopped gabbling on about the man who'd made friends with her just to steal her ox, the cattle rustlers, the thieves who'd stolen her money, the lawyer in Malanje and the mulatto children and all the rest that Don'Ana, Mrs Domingas and the captain like to talk about. But I'm not so sure – when someone's at that stage of blackwater fever, they say things they've never heard nor learnt, nor even passed through their minds. It's just the evil spirits talking.

That's what she had: blackwater fever. She was as yellow as an egg when she arrived, sweating and twisting all over the bed, and if it hadn't been for Mrs Domingas's root medicine and the hot brick they tied to her back, she might well have woken up dead in the morning. But the remedies worked, her pee turned clear again and no longer red with blood, and this cheered everyone up after such a tiring night. She slept like a child, her face turning from yellow back to white, her ample bosom gently rising and falling, and one by one everyone left, thanked by the man in the white suit who shook everyone's hand, trying to laugh, saying 'see you tomorrow, neighbours' and 'good night, friends'.

On the way back to their huts where the children were already fast asleep, it was the things in the suitcase, the house and the shifty look on the man's face, not looking anyone in the eye, that filled the dark night – if it hadn't been for them he'd have let his own wife die, the women said.

'His wife?' Captain Bento interrupted. 'What makes you think that? I spoke to him and, well…'

'But he saw her completely naked when we moved her!'

'And so? Does that mean he's her husband? You women…'

'Look here, just you shut your mouth. You weren't even there.'

They went back over all that business with the brick and that's how the story of the arrival of Dona Garibaldina Ferreira Lemos in our *musseque* ended up. Mind you, we only found out her real name later on because everyone, from Golungo to Malanje and from Canhoca to our *musseque*, called her Albertina Mukuangombe – we'd never even heard Garibaldina used as someone's name before. Even today no one knows who the man was, and Albertina never again spoke about the night she arrived. All we know is what she herself said a couple of days later when the door and windows of her hut opened to reveal the woman already on her feet again, very white and much thinner, but laughing at the fresh morning breeze.

'Dear friends! I'll never be able to thank you enough!' she

called out to the women, driving away any notions about white people's ingratitude. Then she added sadly, 'He left first thing in the morning, that night I got here. I knew he wouldn't be back. Oh well, that's life!'

Albertina asked if they'd come in and help her tidy up. Everything was in a complete mess and no one dared ask any more questions.

So that's how their friendship, which continues to this day, was born in that time of sickness. And if the captain in all his wisdom sometimes interrupts the conversation to explain who the man was, Mrs Domingas cuts him off with a sneer.

'*Sukuama*! For God's sake just shut up, man! All you did was go with the boy to steal the brick from the building site. And now you're the expert on everything?'

So that's the story of when Dona Garibaldina arrived – Albertina Mukuangombe as she was known in Golungo, or just plain Albertina to everyone, even the children, here in our *musseque*.

2

God but it was infuriating seeing Zito strut around after that night in Albertina's bed!

Of course we called him all sorts of names in the days that followed, but he paid no attention. He strutted around like a cock, and wouldn't even rise to the bait when we made fun of him for wearing only cheap sandals rather than proper shoes. His fame had spread even beyond our *musseque* and girls started turning up from all over the place. Tereza and Joanica found themselves besieged by new friends at the Regional Association, and every evening at six o'clock there'd be a bunch of girls who'd decide, just for a change, to go home along Rua da Pedreira rather than up the Calçada da Missão, and so would find themselves passing through our *musseque*. Of course they all pretended they were just keeping Carmindinha company, but we all knew it was really to see Zito. He already had quite a reputation with the girls, and now he'd even been found sleeping in the bed of Albertina, the white woman! Okay, so if you pay, you get what you pay for, the girls said knowingly to each other. But Zito certainly didn't have any money for that. And on it went – entire conversations were made up, all sorts of things Albertina had never said, as the girls made their way through our *musseque*.

'It's true! She says she's never had a man like him!' one of them winked.

Some of the girls giggled at the boldness of it all, while others clapped their hands over their mouths, pretending to be embarrassed or that they didn't understand, or muttering something about telling their mothers.

'Oh, for Christ's sake, stop all that simpering nonsense!' the ringleader told them sharply. 'I bet you've been pushed up against a few walls in your time. You're not fooling anyone!'

The simperers tutted angrily under their breath, but carried on with the rest of the group – they were already near our *musseque*. And there was Zito, acting his usual self, smoking a cigarette, whistling away and pretending not to hear them, until one of the bolder girls finally went up and said hello.

'Well hello there, gorgeous!' he replied with a wink.

The lad's fame kept spreading. The older girls kept on talking about him and Mrs Sessá got more and more worried. Mr Sebastião didn't pay any attention to her and laughed contentedly, basking in the glory of his son.

'Just listen, Bastião! He's still going there. What I'm afraid of is that one day he'll run into a whole battalion of soldiers or whatever, and then what?'

Mr Sebastião shrugged his shoulders. 'With our son? They'd need all their battalions!' he joked.

As for the rest of us, we just stood back and watched him, jealousy raging inside us, but we couldn't really be angry with him. We'd been friends for so long that nothing and nobody was going to spoil it. Zeca even got a beating from his father for still talking to Zito – the proud shoemaker didn't want any son of his hanging around with 'that black scoundrel', as he called him.

Then suddenly the dry season was over.

September came and brought with it the first light rains, and the story about Zito and Albertina, that 'shame on decent people', as Dona Eva kept calling her, gradually faded away; the anger softened and began to melt with the *musseque* itself, as the steadily rising heat drove talk about money problems deep into the night. Life resumed its normal course and every day the wind blew through the huts, rustling the leaves in the trees and raising swirls of dust in the sand.

But Mr Luís was on the lookout, ready to pounce. He'd been seething ever since all that fuss about Nanito shooting Zeca in the backside – even back then Don'Ana had heard him threatening to 'do something' about Albertina. So all this business about Zito reopened old wounds.

'I'm going to clean all the shit out of this *musseque*,' he told the other men drinking in the bar round the back of Mr Antunes's store. 'Just you wait: I, Luís Fonseca, promise to turn this tip into a place fit for civilised people to live in!'

By this stage he was bright red, puffing up his pigeon chest beneath his police shirt and waving his hands around to make his point. Mr Antunes, his belly protruding from under his grubby vest, carried on topping up their glasses.

'And a white woman, too. Imagine that! It's a bloody disgrace,' he added.

He spoke slowly, choosing his words as if he himself couldn't believe what he was saying, watching his friends' hands grasping their glasses, ready to refill them as soon as they were empty. Mr Luís thumped his puny chest and gulped down his drink.

'I'll put an end to it, Antunes. I'll put an end to it, just you see,' he said darkly.

The policeman's burning anger (we heard all about it when we were sent down to the shop later on) and young Zito's fame marched hand in hand, filling the hearts of everyone with fear or delight. Nobody wanted to think about what it all might lead to. Zito still came over to play with us, and, despite all of Zeca's dad's threats, we carried on just as before and our shrieks of laughter put cheerfulness back into the *musseque*'s afternoons. We weren't scared – Zito was our friend and when he was with us, he became a kid again, which is what he still was really. In their backyards, our mothers could hear their children playing happily, and so they put all that talk of malice and fury and vengeance behind them.

That's when it happened.

It was a muggy afternoon of clouds and flies, and very hot. Zito was sitting under the *gajaja* tree and Xoxombo was telling him how Antoninho was still threatening him on the way home from school and that the other day he'd even shouted over that Carmindinha was a whore and was going to turn out like Albertina.

'Bloody hell!' swore Zito. 'And you just let him say things like that about your sister?'

'*Pópilas*! The bastard ran off into his dad's grocery store. But I still chucked a stone at him.'

If Xoxombo wanted, said Zito, he'd pin the little fucker down, nick his clothes and leave him there with his balls hanging out for everyone to see. But Zeca thought it was a bad idea and I agreed. We told Zito that Antoninho was too young for him and that Xoxombo could handle him on his own.

It was still too early to meet up with the girls coming back from sewing, but Zito had already put on his sandals and his hair was sparkling with too much brilliantine. Zeca Bunéu said 'let's go and play football', taking a swing at our half-stuffed ball that would have been more at home on a rubbish heap than a playing field. Zito shook his head. Zeca told him he was just scared of losing, but Zito said it was because he didn't want to get himself dirty. So the best thing to play would be *quigozas*.

I suppose *quigozas* means something like 'joyride', although our version is much the same as piggy-back. It's a *musseque* boy's game – a game for boys who have no toys. You play it during the afternoons when you've had enough of the jar game, when the sun's too hot for kicking a ball around, when you've lost interest in kites and you're fed up driving around in cars made out of cardboard boxes. So, you all find yourselves a big pebble, round or flat according to your own preference. Then you want to make sure you're the last one to throw. Fights usually break out because of this, but eventually someone draws a line with their bare foot in the sand and the guys who are going first throw their pebbles from here. To *quigozar* someone who's already thrown, all you have to do is throw your pebble so that it hits his. If you get him, then he has to carry you on his back from where you're standing to where your pebble ended up. Anyone can play, although of course the weaker ones, as soon as it's their turn to carry someone, try to get out of it and make some excuse about cheating. Then someone punches them and they then run off to tell their mothers. We call it joyriding because, before we made up this version, we used to hang off the backs of vans and lorries when they came through the *musseque* and that was our kind of joyriding. Now we just joyride each other.

We were too caught up in our game, creasing up with laughter when tiny little Xoxombo had to carry big heavy Zito, to notice the trouble brewing in front of our houses down below. Xoxombo had just fallen flat on his face, his mouth full of sand and spitting what looked like blood, so it was me who heard it first.

'Stop, all of you!' I called out. 'Look! Isn't that some sort of argument going on down there?'

Everyone stopped and we all peered down in that direction. We couldn't see very well because of the sun coming out from behind the clouds, but it looked like someone was running away and Albertina was chasing them with a broom. Zeca Bunéu, with his eagle eyes, started to run.

'*Pópilas*!' he exclaimed. 'It's Albertina! She's giving Aníbal Manco a beating!'

The rest of us leapt up like kid goats, shouting that it was a race to get there first. Zito, Xoxombo and I whistled past Zeca, who was rubbish at running. When we arrived, panting, there was fat Mr Aníbal with his lame foot cowering on the ground and Albertina beating him over the head with a broom made out of palm husk.

'Burglar! Thief! So you want to steal my stuff?'

Mrs Domingas and Mrs Sessá came over to help calm their friend down but all her fears, fears that had been building up over weeks of arguments, came flooding out and Albertina was too furious even to listen to them. Dona Branca stood across the street with her husband, one eye trained on Mr Luís standing over in his doorway.

'Do you see that?' she whispered to her husband, loud enough for everyone to hear. 'You're a witness, for goodness' sake! Come on, man – someone's got to put a stop to this nonsense. A fine example to set the children!'

Don'Ana, who couldn't stand the policeman, let Carmindinha and Tunica poke fun at him.

'Look at him just standing there! What an idiot! He's all mouth and no…'

'Now behave yourselves, girls! Children should be seen and not heard!' But Don'Ana was laughing, her eyes gleaming.

Mrs Sessá had managed to get hold of Albertina and was pushing her back towards the house, but she was having none of it. She shook herself free of her friend's embrace and turned back towards the man, shaking her broom at the rent collector.

'Come on, Manco!' she screamed at him. 'Get back over here and I'll give you a good hiding, you worthless piece of shit!'

Mr Aníbal came after her, limping and clutching his tatty old briefcase. Seeing Mr Luís the policeman standing in his doorway, he shouted out that she'd better give him the rent money or he'd throw her out in the street. Those were the boss's orders, and if she didn't have the money, he'd take her gold chain and earrings. At that, Albertina broke free of the hands holding her and lunged at him. The rent man fled, shouting more threats over his shoulder. Then when he reached Mr Luís's doorway and heard what the policeman was saying to Zeca's dad, his courage returned.

'It's not your fault, you filthy old whore!' he shouted over at her. 'It's my boss's fault for renting huts to bloody prostitutes!'

By this stage, we had arrived running and were standing right next to the rent man. But none of us imagined what would happen next: Zito literally flew at him. Dona Eva screamed and Mr Lúis raced off into his backyard. The rent man lay splayed out on the sand – I bet he didn't even know what had hit him. Carmindinha and Tunica clapped their hands and we all burst out laughing, even when Mr Luís, seething with rage, came back out with his whip to thrash Zito. But Zito had already gone. From a distance, shaking the sand from his hair and shorts, he laughed at the policeman and made rude signs with his fingers. Mr Aníbal was back on his feet, brushing down his briefcase.

'You've got no right,' he complained. 'A sick man like me and you all just stand there laughing? Well, just you wait – I'm going to press charges. You haven't heard the end of this. Officer – did you see what they did?'

Hearing the question, Mr Luís laughed his evil laugh and came over to give him his hand, just like they were old friends from years ago.

'Don't worry, Aníbal,' he said, leading the old man towards his hut. 'I saw the whole thing. Come in and clean yourself up, man! You and I are going to clear out all the filth from this *musseque*!'

The afternoon raced towards its end. A cold wind from nowhere curled round the people standing about, taken aback by Mr Luís's joviality as he took the man into his own house. Slowly, silently, they came and stood around Albertina, who was sitting on her doorstep. They wanted to cheer her up, but in their hearts they knew that if Mr Luís and Aníbal Manco combined forces, well, that was that. She was already two months in arrears, all that time in hospital had taken it out of her and there were no more letters from Malanje. How was she going to make ends meet?

'Come on, Albertina. No need to cry – we'll help you out.'

But cry she did. She cried and cried, and for the first time they heard her take pity on herself – no money to pay the rent, no letters from Malanje, and now the police were throwing her out of her hut.

As for Zito, he'd already headed off down to wait for the girls – these kinds of scenes only interested him when people were throwing punches. Zeca and I felt sorry for Albertina – she was our friend but there was nothing we could do. We left Mrs Domingas, Don'Ana and Mrs Sessá to console her and went over to Xoxombo, who'd stopped crying now his sisters were with him.

Helped by the soothing words of her friends, Albertina began to calm down. Don'Ana even promised to go downtown and speak to Aníbal Manco's boss – he'd have to listen to her, after all she was Floriano Pinheiro's widow. And when the crippled old rent collector nervously left the policeman's house as night began to shroud our *musseque* in shadows, Albertina had recovered enough to throw one last jibe.

'Well, look who it is! I suppose he let you have a go with his wife too, then? Filthy old half-caste!'

But suddenly she shut up. Mr Luís was standing in his doorway, whistling like no one had ever heard him whistle before. That cold wind returned, cutting like a knife through all the women, and Albertina shrank back.

'Oh, sisters!' she whispered. 'This time I really am finished!'

The others tried saying all the usual things: that they were her friends, they'd help her, she just needed some peace and calm, there was no way they could run her out of her own house and home, but nothing they said could calm Albertina's doubts and fears. Even after nightfall she stayed there sitting on her doorstep, stroking and talking to her mongrel.

'*Aiuê*! So then, *Nameless*, what's to become of me?' she said, shaking her head. 'Only Zito can help me. He's the only one.'

3

Albertina left just a few months after we carried our dear friend Xoxombo to the old cemetery.

They were our last school holidays together. Zeca and I would soon be off to the high school and Carmindinha said fearfully that soon I'd forget all about her, meet loads of pretty schoolgirls and wouldn't want to go out with a girl from the *musseque* any more. That made me angry. Other than messages through Tunica, we went for weeks without speaking, but we spent the whole time furtively looking at each other – it didn't seem possible to live without each other's eyes.

There'd never been holidays as sad as these – even carnival couldn't lift our spirits. Biquinho was gone, Zito was back in jail because of the Aníbal Manco thing, and poor little Xoxombo was lying there in the cemetery – we went there every Sunday with Tunica and Carmindinha to lay flowers. No one wanted to play with their catapults any more or even set traps, and Mrs Sessá had let Zito's canaries fly away. With just me and Zeca now, I would lie there holding my old conch shell to my ear and listen to the sound of the sea from when I'd been a little boy down in Coqueiros.

Things carried on quietly in the *musseque*, every day a little sadder. We hardly saw Mrs Domingas any more, and Captain Abano had gone off on a voyage up north. The only signs of life were Zeca's dad whistling as he hammered the shoe leather into shape and the comings and goings of Aníbal Manco, who was now great friends with Mr Luís. Albertina had aged suddenly and spent the whole time sitting on her doorstep talking to her dog and waiting, for who or what no one knew. Some days she'd wander over to help Mrs Sessá or

Don'Ana with their housework – Don'Ana's little girls, Tété and Bebiana, were getting bigger now and all they wanted to do was run around in the backyard playing at getting their clothes dirty.

I remember it like it was yesterday. It was a bright, sunny April morning and I was sitting on my doorstep when I heard, far away, that sound I'll never forget: the whistle call of our *musseque*. Then came Zito's song – the song he'd learnt in jail and that sometimes I'd forgetfully sing to Carmindinha. I ran over and called out to Zeca for him to come quickly, and that's when we saw our friend standing tall and strong as a man up by the baobab tree, silhouetted against the sky. Just hearing his voice filled our hearts with happiness.

> *Wandering through the bananas*
> *Two lovers getting hot*
> *The lad's getting close, the lad's getting close*
> *No harm done…*

'*Pópilas!*' exclaimed Zeca. 'He hasn't forgotten his old song! Can you hear?'

Yes, I could hear. It was Zito, singing the song he'd learnt from that 'Sugarman' guy he was always going on about. I could tell that even with the holidays coming to an end, the good times were back. Once again, we'd go and catch canaries to put in a cage, or even clear off for the whole afternoon and go fishing and diving off the rocks at Mãe-Isabel, like I'd been wanting to do for so long.

'Hey, Zito!'

'Hey, Zeca!'

We grabbed hold of our friend and pulled him away from the angry, tearful embraces of Mrs Sessá and the advice

Don'Ana had already started giving him – she wouldn't even let the poor boy sit down and eat the *matete* porridge his mother had served up. Mrs Domingas, even in her sadness, was there too. Tunica and Carmindinha had come, and our squabbles evaporated with the happiness of Zito coming home. To everyone's surprise even Dona Branca appeared, with the excuse of needing to speak to Zeca.

'So then, Mrs Sessá,' she said calmly, turning to Zito's mother. 'I'm sure you're much happier now! What we all need now is for this bad boy to learn a bit of sense!'

Zito laughed and said he had a lot of sense; what he didn't have was luck, and when someone is born with bad luck the best thing to do is nothing, or else whatever you do only brings the bad luck down on top of you. He carried on laughing, then turned the subject around and said to Mrs Domingas how sorry he was about Xoxombo. He was a real man now, not like the rest of us who always wanted to say something about Xoxombo but could never get the words out. Tears ran down her wide face, even more wrinkled than before, and we could hear the deep sadness in Zito's voice.

'Good kid, Xoxombo. No one quite like him, mama. And he's up there in heaven, mama – the only place he's gone is heaven.'

Everybody nodded. Yes sir, a kid as smart and good as Xoxombo was bound to be an angel. Quiet kid, never did anyone any harm. While the conversation went on like this, Zeca stayed silent – he knew that when Mrs Domingas and Don'Ana said these things they were thinking about those stories of his that had made Xoxombo the talk of the whole *musseque*. It was Zito who rescued him, launching back into his prison tales – hunger, thirst, working on the roads, beatings from the guards – but even as he talked about it, he didn't look angry or sad. He just talked normally, saying Xoxombo was a good kid and then telling his mother all this jail stuff wasn't too bad, and yes, that's when we realised that Zito was now a man.

Albertina was the last to arrive. She'd done her hair, put on a clean dress, her face was smiling and she embraced Zito warmly. She talked and asked questions, and everyone could see written on everyone else's face that the *musseque*'s secret was no longer a secret, and that everyone was only pretending not to know that Zito was sleeping with Albertina whenever he wanted, and that Albertina liked having him in her bed.

'The only thing I was afraid of was that, by the time I got out, Mr Luís would already have sent you packing!'

Albertina laughed. 'What, him? He's a big pussycat now!'

Don'Ana wasn't having any of it. 'Don't joke about it, Albertina. You'll see. He's a monster, that man. You mark my words, a monster. Why's he always talking to Aníbal? Tell me that.'

'I don't know, sister. But what I've heard is that he's going to buy my hut off him.'

Mrs Domingas roused herself from her unhappy silence. 'That's what Bento says,' she said, almost as if it wasn't her talking. 'Seems he's bought your hut to build himself a new house.'

'Well they'll have to get me out first! That's what he wants, sister Domingas – that's what it's all about!'

It could well be true what people were saying in our *musseque*. Ever since Mr Augusto had been thrown out of his hut, lots of things were pointing in that direction. More and more new roofs were creeping across the grass and scrub, eating away at the sands, and every month that passed you could feel the city inching its way towards us. Rumbling lorries of gravel and sand appeared from all around while workmen dug ditches and filled them with stones. Brightly coloured new houses, with verandas at the front and flowers in the garden, trampled over the old huts of mud and sticks. Sheets of corrugated iron lay scattered on the ground amidst the mess of broken reeds and clay, and people with all their belongings piled on their heads and backs fled the clouds of dust, making their way up through the sandy wasteland towards Rangel, Marçal, Sambizanga and beyond.

Nowadays that was all the women here talked about. Even Dona Branca announced that they'd be moving, for good, to the plots up at Km 14. Of course it would be a bit of a bore what with Zeca being down at the high school – he'd need a bicycle, or maybe they'd buy a little van to take the vegetables to market and run him down to school. 'But it all costs money, ladies, and as you all know very well, we certainly aren't rich…'

'Oh I do indeed, Dona Branca!' replied Mrs Domingas. 'But you'll have the vegetable plot, you can work and your husband has money. What'll we do? If Bento has to stop working, how are we going to live? Everything's so expensive now, and I want those girls of mine to get an education.'

Don'Ana nodded in agreement. She was lucky having those two huts over in Bairro Operário that her husband left her when he died. The rent would put Tété and Bebiana through school.

'I promised him on his death bed, and so help me God I'll keep my word. They'll go to the high school and everything.'

The conversation carried on: how would their children manage with everything so expensive, while Mrs Sessá just sat in silence thinking about Sebastião. Right this minute he was clambering up scaffolding on building sites downtown, and every week it was Mr Antunes in the grocery store who took more and more of his wages. Then there was Zito, already a man and not an ounce of sense in him. Better not even to think about it. She made her excuses saying it was time to get lunch ready and went out into the yard. The others went off to do the same.

Time was passing quickly, Zito setting his traps and laying his bait. Bento came back from his voyage a happier man; he loved the sea and seeing all those new places up north helped soothe the sadness of Xoxombo's death. When the weather was fine he'd sit out in the evenings with Mrs Domingas and their neighbours, playing with Bebiana. She was his favourite, a pretty little girl with big, wide eyes and skin the colour of toasted almonds. The grown-ups used to say she looked just like her father, Mr Floriano Pinheiro, although I never knew him and no one would ever tell me anything about him, not even Don'Ana.

There were lots of days when Zito still played with us and our old happiness returned, even though there were only three of us. But nothing was quite the same. He was already a man and he'd often get bored and call us little boys. What he really wanted to do was go out and strut his stuff for the girls coming back from sewing. Then, at night, when it was late and our *musseque* was asleep, he'd jump over the wall and slip into Albertina's bed.

All of this we understood and forgave. But as for his new friendship, well, nobody knew what that was all about. Everyone talked about it and he never explained, not even to his mother. Yes, that friendship was betrayal.

'I just don't understand, sister. He never used to hang around with him!' sighed Mrs Sessá.

It was true. People remembered all the fuss about Zeca Bunéu and the air rifle, when Mr Luís said he'd whip Nanito if he carried on playing with us, and so his only friend here in the *musseque* was Antoninho, Mr Antunes's son down at the grocery store. So how come then, all of a sudden, Zito was coming down the street with his arm around Nanito, completely ignoring both of us and heading off with him to go hunting? Then in the afternoon he'd be round at Nanito's house. At first they'd sit at the front door playing cards, but a few days later, Dona Eva said he could come into the backyard. Not sure what to make of it, the neighbours told Mrs Sessá. But she said she didn't know any more than they did – Zito wouldn't talk about it.

'So what?' he'd replied rudely when she asked. 'Can't I be friends with whoever I want?'

We could feel the anger rising in our chests. Zito had swapped us for Nanito, that scheming little toerag who'd fired an air rifle into Zeca's backside. For goodness' sake, Zito himself had once even wrecked Nanito and Antoninho's stupid raffle!

Yes, the two of them used to run this raffle underneath the *gajaja* tree, with little statues of saints, pictures, bars of soap, books and all sorts of things, and people passing by on their way to or from work would stop and buy tickets for a few cents each. Often they'd win, and Nanito would show them the list and those who knew how to read could see that there were good prizes on the list, but afterwards they'd always come away grumbling about the money and the good prizes never coming up – sometimes they got nothing at all, just blanks.

'*Sukuama*!' they swore. 'Fifty cents and all for nothing! Cheating little rascals…'

And now he's Nanito's best friend? After all that happened? Well, we certainly hadn't forgotten! Zito went with us, Xoxombo was there and Biquinho too. We bought all the tickets we could get for one *angolar* – an old green bank-note with a buffalo head and big horns on it that I'd found down at the old rubbish dump. Every ticket, every single one, drew a blank. Nanito and Antoninho just laughed in our faces at how they'd tricked us.

'Blacks just aren't lucky!' Antoninho crowed.

So how on earth could he be friends with them now? It was Zito himself who started with the kicks, smashing the pictures and little bottles of watered-down perfume, scattering the magazines and statues of saints, calling Nanito and Antoninho thieves just out to swindle people with their stinking raffle, stealing poor people's money just like Antoninho's dad with his grocery store. They wanted a fight – there were two of them and they were feeling strong – so it was us who had to hold them back, calm things down and help them set up the raffle table again. Antoninho was crying with rage, but Zito wasn't going to shut up.

'Okay, I get it,' he seethed. 'Everyone steals. Well I just want to smash all this crap to pieces!'

And now just look at him – sauntering by, arm around the guy's shoulder, spending the whole afternoon sifting through rubbish heaps looking for razor blade wrappers for Nanito's collection! Even worse – and this is what shocked us even more and I said so to Carmindinha – he'd even stopped going down to wait for the girls coming out of sewing school at six o'clock. Instead, he'd stay and help Nanito stick the razor blade wrappers into his scrapbook, sometimes even staying on to have his dinner with him. The three old friends and neighbours, Mrs Domingas, Don'Ana and Mrs Sessá, discussed the mystery among themselves.

'Let it be, sister, just let it be,' said Mrs Sessá, shaking her head sadly. 'Nobody eats him and the boy gets to eat. White people like that sort of thing. Just let it be.'

Meanwhile the cool season was approaching, the sun growing weaker and the days shorter as the rains fled with the high clouds. The chatter of conversation had gone and only sadness and mystery remained in the *musseque*. The women had grown tired of talking – it didn't do any good. You could read in people's faces what they thought about this new friendship of Zito's. Even Mr Luís the policeman was talking to him now, saying let bygones be bygones and that men cast aside these boyish pranks when they learn a bit of sense.

People began to accept that this was how things were going to be, and that the new friendship might even bring a bit of peace to our *musseque*. Zeca's dad even spoke to Captain Bento, although what he said (that if the black youngsters were all as polite to the whites, then they might even grow up into decent men and women) certainly wasn't what the captain wanted to hear. But then, just as things were settling down, a new crisis broke out. No one could make head nor tail of it. Some said it was all a lie and that Mr Luís had invented the whole thing. Others started blaming Zito again, saying he was a lost cause and was back at his old thieving tricks. Dona Branca said it was Albertina's fault and that she'd put him up to it. Albertina swore that the policeman was trying to trap Zito into giving whatever evidence he needed to run her out of the *musseque*.

We only found out when they told us the next morning, scolding and threatening us like somehow it was our fault. And even if the whole thing were true, there was no sign of Zito in his house, and for many weeks we didn't know what we really felt about it – anger at Mr Luís and Nanito or pleased with Zito, even though he'd dumped all of us and made friends with the little bastard who'd fired a lead pellet into Zeca Bunéu's backside.

Zito had tried to steal all of Mr Luís's money. He used a key he'd got hold of one of those times he'd been hanging out with Nanito and slipped, in that leopard way of his, into the policeman's house one dark, moonless, starlit night while the *musseque* was silently sleeping. He'd have got away scot-free if Nanito hadn't still been awake. But the boy's shouts of alarm and Zito banging into the chairs spoilt everything. Mr Luís caught him red-handed with the sweet tin from behind the wardrobe where he hid the money for building the new house.

In the darkness of the night nobody heard the blows – Zito didn't utter a single cry or shout as Mr Luís laid into him. But when Nanito saw him being marched off, he broke down and started bawling. So that's what woke up the whole *musseque*, and there were many people who saw Zito, in the firm grip of Mr Luís and his head hanging in shame, disappear along the path through the long grass.

A week later, a letter arrived at Mr Antunes's grocery store. It was addressed to Don'Ana and put an end to the mystery of Zito's arrest. It was from Albertina. She asked for her friends' forgiveness for not saying goodbye that night when Mr Luís took Zito. She'd realised the lad had tried to rob the policeman to help her pay her rent and she'd been scared out of her wits, so she'd packed her bags and headed straight for the Cidade Alta train station. Now she was living with her son, the one who was applying to join the administrative corps down in Malanje. With her heartfelt apologies and eternal thanks she begged them to take the things in her house – they could all take whatever they wanted, except for her dog *Nameless* who she wanted me to have. But the letter arrived too late – by the time it got here, Aníbal Manco, with Mr Luís and Mr Antunes as his witnesses, had already cleared out all her belongings and carted them off to his boss in lieu of rent.

Even if he drove us mad with all his obsessions, Zito's departure left us with heavy hearts. Time passed very slowly and Mrs Sessá only found out much later on – well into the cool season as the picks and shovels tore open the red sand of our *musseque* where Mr Luís was building his new house on the site of Albertina's hut – that Zito was never coming back. From jail he'd been sent to the work camps in São Tomé, and even today I don't know if he stayed there, if he died or if he came back, because his mum and dad also went away, to live in Cayatte, and we never saw them again.

So it was with all of this heaviness in our hearts that Zeca Bunéu and I started at the high school.

*

Today I look sadly across the red sand, scorched by the sun between the trees and patches of grass running over towards Cinco, Kinaxixi and Bairro Operário, but all the kids and all our childhood games are gone.

It's at times like this that I remember the sea. I sneak in and take the conch from my stepmother's dressing table. The pink and yellow shell really belongs to me – I was the one who found it in the shoals down in the bay and brought it with me when I came to live up here in the *musseque*. I hold it to my ear and it's like a magic spell – I can hear the waves gently pushing and pulling against the sand in front of the Nazaré church, the zigzagging fishermen's canoes, and my old friends Augusto and Carlos down in Coqueiros. We're sitting on the green rocks at Mãe-Isabel, the sun beating down, and I can hear Augusto (who we always called 'Duck' because of the way he dived) calling to us.

'Sissies! It's shallow – come on!'

154

I dive in. He was older than us and had taught us how to swim with one arm holding the fishing line aloft in order to free the hook from where it had got stuck in the rocks, how to sit down and sleep on the seabed, or how to follow the sandbank at low tide right across to the church on the island across the bay.

Inside the shell the wind blows through the palm trees on the island, the red sun slips behind the São Miguel Fort, and in Luanda Bay the sea, our sea, a calm, multi-coloured sea, whispers softly to the sand.

That's what I see when I hold the big conch to my ear. Or sometimes, when I feel like it, I put other people inside the shell. It doesn't matter even if they're afraid of the sea – I can take them diving with Duck and me in our calm, warm sea. I put Xoxombo who's in the old cemetery, Zito who they sent off to São Tomé, Biquinho who moved away, and even Zeca who's gone off with his dad on his new bike to water the vegetable plot up at Km 14.

I'm all alone in our *musseque*, watching the red sand baking in the late afternoon sun between the trees and patches of grass all the way down to Bungo, Ingombota and Cabeça. The others aren't coming to play any more and there's no more stopping by at Albertina's door for some sweet *kikuerra* or the other tasty things she always used to give us.

I'm just waiting for Zeca Bunéu. As usual, he'll be coming over later for us to write our newspaper together, just like when it was all still a game that Captain Abano taught us. But now we're studying at the high school and clinging on, alone, in our empty *musseque*.

Carmindinha and Me

VIII

It's like I can still hear Tunica singing under the cassava bush in the backyard, in that sweet voice of hers that gradually grew and ripened.

> *On Sunday I went to Kifangondo*
> *In Kifangondo there was no water...*

Then she'd stop washing the clothes and take a few steps, the same little dance she'd often do on her way to fetch water. Mrs Domingas wasn't impressed.

'So then, Tunica,' she said angrily, 'is this what you call working?'

Tunica would turn round and laugh, suck the air through her teeth in mock irritation and carry on singing.

> *The soup*
> *The soup was rich*
> *With water from the ditch*

Now all we have is a postcard with shining white, square-shaped houses all jumbled up together, lettering nobody can understand, a stamp no one can read and Tunica's rushed handwriting, rounded like her own body, filling the little piece of thin white card. 'Everything's fine. One of these days I'll write a letter. This place is pretty and I like it. Please don't think I'm unhappy. Don't worry, mum – I'm fine here even though lots of times it's really cold.' Things like that, and other stuff.

Mrs Domingas cried as she looked at the card. She couldn't make any sense of it, but it was Tunica she was holding in her hands – the same hands, old and wrinkled now from the washtub and stove, that had washed her and dressed her and smacked her and mended her tunic to go to school. That's when she asked us never to put Tunica's story in our newspaper. And when I solemnly swore we wouldn't, Carmindinha came and stood beside me and we just stood there, silently watching her mother weep. Even Zeca kept his mouth shut.

Tangier. That was the name of the city where Tunica was, singing and dancing her rumbas and sambas. That's all we knew. 'Tónia the Blonde and Her Friends' was what Antoninho reported from Lisbon, and Mr Antunes made sure the shameful gossip reached Mrs Domingas's ears. The old captain hid hunched and silent in the corner reading his paper, not speaking and not leaving the house. When he went off on one of his voyages, he just stared silently at the sea that had robbed him of his Tunica.

Later on, when Bento died, with Mrs Xica's house demolished by the bulldozer, Mrs Sessá loading up her belongings and leaving for Cayatte with a heart worn out by all that had happened with Zito, and Albertina just a memory every morning when the workers' train whistles six-thirty from the Cidade Alta station, Mrs Domingas and Carmindinha also made their way across the red sands, fleeing, like everyone else, from the memories of our *musseque*.

But no one could forget. Even if she moved to other lands or even another country, everything was still written on those roughened hands, those shrivelled breasts that had once been full, those creases of her dark face down which tears now flowed, that hair whitening from its roots steeped in all those stories of life deep inside her head, and in her stubborn beating heart that still remembers things she wants to forget, and which listens when Zeca and me and Carmindinha talk, but sometimes doesn't want to hear.

And in that little house, far away from our *musseque*, the portrait of ship's master Bento de Jesus Abano, Captain Abano as we always called him, hangs on the wall. He looks at us from beneath his sailor's cap with his quiet smile, and it's our sea – blue, green, grey and white, mixed with yellow and brown from the great rivers that flow into it – that we can see. Beaches yellow in the sun, hills, red and chalk-white, running along the coast and swathes of green from the rains covering up our sadness at not having him with us any more, sitting reading quietly in his corner, carefully explaining how a newspaper works, arguing with Carmindinha and patiently implanting in us a love of our country.

Old Mrs Domingas is dozing in her chair and Zeca, in a low voice, with the portrait's permission, starts telling Carmindinha (who hadn't been there) about that trip we'd taken back in the school holidays, years ago.

The old yellowing portrait reaches down from the wall and holds the helm of Zeca Bunéu's imagination so he doesn't drift off course like he usually does. Carmindinha and I lose ourselves in the beaches of his story, holding hands and seeking out a cool, green place to lay our heads, because that truly is what our love is like.

1

Zeca Bunéu talks and we listen. Carmindinha by my side, Mrs Domingas sleeping in the chair. As he talks, I can see it all once again: the little white boat shuddering in the stiff southerly breeze, its bow dipping through the waves, blue crests and green underneath, yawning lazily then thrusting forward, baring their foamy white teeth and rolling in on themselves along the yellow line of beach. The wet sand shimmering in the sun and the sky so blue we couldn't tell where it joined the sea. Ropes creaking in the salt wind, shrouds, masts straining in the sun and, lambasted by Maneco Santo, the crew hauling in the billowing yellowed canvas of the main sail before changing tack.

Both of us were terrified. Captain Bento stood smiling at the helm, his taut, sun-beaten muscles holding the *Good Journey* on course as she leaned over, slapping her white belly against the waves, a little ripple of laughter running along her keel from bow to stern, then righting herself and veering back towards land, straight towards the green hills clothed in their new grass where Maneco Santo's sharp eyes were already pointing out the fort, the high school and the hospital, although we couldn't make out any of it.

Nearer the shore, the sea was dark brown from the red mud and the grass, stretching like a long stain in our wake. Maneco Santo explained that it was the waters of the Kwanza, a river so big that boats sail on it just like the sea. He told us that it rises high up in Bié Province, runs north towards Malanje, but then changes its mind, no one knows why, and turns angrily westwards, eating its way through rocks and hillsides and thick forests, tearing up trees and earth and then, sensing the sea from the winds that feed it with rain, races towards the ocean. Maneco Santo said, and we believed him, that the great river only rested when it reached Dondo and felt the sea mingling in its waters. Even then it pushed on towards the coast – big, broad and powerful, but tamed, its anger gone.

Zeca and I laughed, hanging onto the ropes and watching the flying fish circling round us like birds. The captain handed the helm over to Maneco and came forward to explain to us that they grew fins almost like wings so they could fly over the waves – sometimes they even landed in the boat or went right over it from one side to the other.

And once again, closer now, there was the whisper of the waves pulling on the sand of the beach. It sounded so gentle, but we could tell it was just a mask for the anger of the ocean swell. Bento Abano swore that it was the most beautiful island in the world and he pointed to the coconut trees swaying in the wind like they were dancing to the rhythm of a *dicanza,* the houses interspersed with mango trees laden with red and yellow fruit, the fishermen's nets, small dark outcrops of rock poking through the lush green grass, people's huts almost lost among the colours. The sea, our sea, pounded the shore, running right up the beach like it was some kind of game, covering up all the shimmering yellow sand and stroking the edge of the grass with its white foamy fingers. Then it roared with laughter and whisked back the covers to reveal the glistening, naked, white shells lying underneath. Smaller waves bounced off the trawler's bow, covering everything again like they didn't want the game to end, and the sun looked down from high up above where it commanded, along with the moon still hidden beyond the horizon, the comings and goings of the tides, just like Captain Abano had taught us.

The loosened bow jib flapped furiously in the wind and the

crew leapt forward to haul it in, Maneco Santo barking at them from the main deck.

'Never met a man quite like him for giving orders,' said Bento, wistfully.

With her sails trimmed, the *Good Journey* leant further over and began to tack closer to the wind, the sound of the sea louder in our ears as it slapped against the white wall of the hull. The noise came back to us again that night and Zeca said it sounded like someone talking, which made me think of mermaids in books.

When night came, there was a pitch black sky running into a sea full of stars. Our old friend the captain came and sat with us up in the bow, staring at the sky and telling us names we'd never heard of and which made us laugh.

'So how's that Taurus, then?' asked Zeca. 'Where are its horns?'

Bento Abano showed us others too, told us their names, and each time we laughed. For such beautiful things, why did people give them such ugly names as 'Big Dog' and 'Little Dog'? And what on earth was 'Pleiades'? I kept my mouth shut, but Zeca went on asking questions and Captain Bento explained patiently, again and again, that the stars don't move and that they're like our own sun but much, much bigger. He pointed and said 'Sirius', but even he couldn't explain what that one meant.

It was Maneco Santo who showed me my favourite ones: four of them, far astern of us, tilting over and almost falling into the sea. One of them was shining so brightly I said it was Carmindinha, and Maneco laughed. They looked like a wonky, lopsided kite, I said. Maneco Santo agreed, but said the men who'd given them a name had never played with kites so they'd called them something else. When he told me the name

I shouted out that I already knew it, the captain and Zeca came over and that's what led to the conversation about newspapers.

It was the Southern Cross. I'd heard the name but had no idea it had anything to do with the stars. I had of course read those old newspapers the captain kept hidden away and didn't like us touching just in case we tore them. So this was the Southern Cross. Zeca was listening to the captain going on about newspapers back in the olden days, so I was the only one who heard Maneco Santo explain that the star in the kite's tail always pointed south and that it gave sailors their true bearings so they wouldn't get lost on stormy nights. I could see why the paper had chosen it for a name and why the captain liked it so much.

Zeca and I didn't sleep at all that night. We stayed awake until the sun came up, watching the sea and sky turn exactly the same colour, the green coconut trees and shimmering white sands fringing Mussulo Bay and, far in the distance, the first of the fishermen's skiffs drowsily cutting through the waves with sails made from old sugar sacks. As we headed northwards, our little boat picked up speed as it caught the scent of the calm, restful waters of Luanda Bay.

But Captain Abano didn't want to change the subject. Now there were just the two of us, he said, the best thing to do would be to make up our own newspaper, telling the stories of our *musseque.* Zeca could even publish some of those poems he was writing. When we got home, he promised he'd let us look at the *Southern Cross, The Angolan* and some of the other old newspapers that had things written by him in them.

Once again, the flying fish were leaping around the white belly of the boat, its curved bow slicing through the water and its mast leaning towards our very own Luanda Island, already clearly in view. Maneco Santo and the crew got everything ready so they could land quickly and get off home to their families. Swaying gently with the movement of his boat, the old captain held the helm with his usual steady calm and carried on talking to us, planting firmly in our minds the idea of a newspaper. Zeca was already promising to write about our voyage, with a full description of the *Good Journey*, the captain, the stars and everything else.

Holding the helm in his left hand, Captain Bento pointed down into the glassy, blue water on the other side of the deck. You could see almost right to the bottom, where shoals of fish raced alongside us.

'Mullet. Thousands of them. Our sea has everything!' The captain wasn't speaking to anyone in particular; his words were for everyone. 'And if I'd taken you further on down to Baía Farta, Moçâmedes and beyond, you'd have seen even more!'

Curious as ever, Zeca went over to take a closer look at the fish. I stayed beside the captain, his calm, steady voice teaching me about the richness of our sea, rich with more fish than I could imagine – Bento said there were millions of them.

'Even whales?'

The captain smiled and took off his cap to wipe away the sweat. And then, just like he was my own dad, he put his hand on my shoulder.

'Yes, everything,' he whispered in my ear. 'Humpback whales, sperm whales, dolphins, you name it. Do you remember that time a really big whale came ashore and died, right here in our bay?'

He said some names I already knew and others I'd never heard of. His voice was different when he spoke their names, like when he told us about Taurus, the Big Dog and Sirius, or when he talked about the *Good Journey,* about the sands of

Mussulo Bay twinkling in the sun, palm trees wafting in the breeze, cascading ravines of silky grass, Cape Island, Chicala, Corimba, Samba and everything else. You could tell Captain Bento loved these things in a way no one else in our *musseque* knew about – I could see it in his wrinkled eyes, almost hidden under the dark shadow of his peaked cap, always looking ahead to where the sea and the sky and our beautiful land joined together. He smiled just like a child, or like one of those saints in the church at the São Paulo Mission, and when he put his hand on my shoulder I could sense everything he was feeling flow down his arm and into my heart. I looked around me the way the captain had taught me, at the waves laughing in the foamy depths of Corimba, at the shoals of fish, at the sunlight falling on the stark, naked roofs of our city, at the green hands of the palm trees on the island waving cheerily at the *Good Journey,* the captain's faithful travelling companion from Walvis Bay to the Congo, Chiloango and beyond, right up to the green, shark-infested seas of São Tomé and the little isle of Príncipe.

When we got back to our *musseque*, everyone said Zeca and I looked sad and kept asking if it hadn't been fun, if we hadn't enjoyed the trip. Only the captain understood that it was happiness we were suffering from, because we wanted to get started on our newspaper so that everyone could read about the love we felt when the wind rattles through the coconut trees on the islands, by the sea, in our land.

2

Night fell quickly that Saturday, almost as if the sky itself was afraid of the sullen anger that lurked everywhere in people's eyes. And although it wasn't so hot now that the rains were nearly over, the sweat poured from everyone's bodies when they started talking about the trouble in the *musseques*. Some people said the soldiers showed no respect and were out to pick a fight, while the whites snarled back that the troops were quite right and those blacks needed to be taught a thing or two. But all that talking came later. A couple of street vendors on the Calçada da Missão were beaten up by three soldiers. Families complained about soldiers banging on their doors at all hours of the day and night wanting to know where they could buy a woman. Mothers started bringing their daughters indoors earlier – these men would grope anything they passed by, and it didn't matter how old or young she was. People shook their heads when they heard about the old man in Terra-Nova who'd come out of his house to defend his daughter – they'd beaten him with their cartridge belts, then run off through the long grass and were never seen again. Even further down, in Ingombota and Bungo, worried mothers and fathers watched anxiously as soldiers wandered around in groups, looking and laughing threateningly.

With all these stories flying around, the girls started coming home from work earlier, setting off from downtown with fear in their stomachs. People were getting angrier. The attacks increased. Many times a soldier would lie bleeding on a street corner, his head gashed by a stone or a barrel hoop that had appeared out of the night from nowhere. No one saw, knew or heard anything about it. Doors were bolted, and the only sound was the creaking of army boots on sand as a heavy silence descended on the abandoned streets.

It was like the coming of the rains – black clouds climb menacingly above the shacks, a fierce gust tears up the sand, then the wind drops suddenly and, after a brief moment of silence, thunder bursts out across the sky, lightning slices

168

through the clouds setting fire to the cashew tree where some poor soul is sheltering, and the rain comes pelting down on the tin roofs. And so on that Saturday that no one could forget, amidst all the fear and anger welling up inside us, there flashed the glint of a small, sharp penknife.

A soldier lay dead, stone dead, in broad daylight, right there in the city centre in full view of everyone passing by, his belly sliced open by the blade of a street vendor selling sweet *kikuerra* and *mikondos*, his guts spilling out over the tarmac and his blood running dark like the first streams of water when the rains begin.

News flew like the wind through the city, and in our *musseque* everyone locked themselves in their houses. Dona Branca even slammed the door in Carmindinha's face when she went round to look for Zeca, and Mr Luís the policeman went out, in full view of everyone, to clean his pistol in the backyard and take a pot shot at the baobab tree. In some of the other *musseques*, the seething anger ran as far as hands and fingertips that reached for old knives and machetes, and behind their closed doors everyone listened anxiously to the sound of boots. All night the soldiers came pouring through the *musseques*, shouting, firing shots, banging on doors, and fear stalked the hearts of the people hiding inside their homes.

And so the night passed, measured by footsteps and silence. Sunday began differently, strangely. Even though it was still the end of the hot season and the sun rose yellow, almost white, everything seemed somehow cooler, calmer. Sparrows sang from the branches of trees, shaking the morning light from their feathers, but no one listened to them, or even noticed. The sound of the soldiers' boots still rang in our ears, driving out what little faith the new day brought.

Just before eight o'clock, Mrs Domingas ventured out

with Carmindinha to go to mass at the São Paulo Mission. Carmindinha went over to get Zeca – Mrs Domingas didn't want to run into his dad since he'd been going around saying that the soldiers were quite right to throw a few punches here and there.

Zeca Bunéu came out in his shorts, his hair caked with brilliantine. Dona Branca always put it on to tame his porcupine hair, as Pexilas the barber called it, although that was just making excuses for his viciously blunt old clippers. My stepmother told me to be careful and together we set off on the path towards Kinaxixi as if nothing had happened and it was just another ordinary day. Captain Abano came to the door to see us off – he was staying behind to look after Tunica, who was sick. He'd go and get his paper later on when we came back from mass.

Like I said, it was one of those clear, bright Sundays you get at the end of the rainy season. The light streamed in through the tall windows of the Mission, reaching even the altar. When we came to the bit where Father Neves and the sacristan turned to face the congregation, they looked like saints with light shining from their heads. I don't think I'll ever forget that light – maybe I remember it because I liked watching Father Neves and hearing him say with his fixed smile and fixed hands all those words in Latin my stepmother wanted me to learn too. That's when the first stone smashed through the stained glass and the sun flooded in even brighter than before, accompanied by the sound of boots scraping against the concrete at the door of the church. If I remember it so clearly it's because at that precise moment I was stealing a glance at Carmindinha, trying to catch her smile. And so I saw the terror in her eyes as fear swept through the church, crushing the kneeling congregation and extinguishing the peace of the mass at the exact moment when, bathed in sleepy sunlight, Father Neves lifted up the chalice and smiled his saintly smile.

The women leapt up in fear and pulled their children towards the altar. The men wanted to go outside into the street, but from that direction came the sound of crowds of clamouring voices scraping their barrel hoops like scythes against the walls, while inside the church, stones and stained glass flew through the air and sunlight rained down on the saints and the altar. Father Neves raised his voice, trying to reassure people.

'Keep calm, everybody! Please, everyone, for the love of God!'

He set down the chalice and came forward towards us with his thin little arms raised, waving his bony hands to say there was nothing to worry about, that it was all some sort of misunderstanding. He tried to go over and talk to the soldiers, who were now huddled in the back corner beside the holy water. But the sacristan, seeing the soldiers pull off their ammunition belts and start rolling them up in their hands, shouted out what everyone was thinking.

'Help! They're going to kill us!'

There was absolutely nothing Father Neves could do. The women shrieked, grabbed their children in their arms and ran, tripping over their long African robes, pushing their way towards the side door and watching in terror as the soldiers leapt over the pews and the stones put paid to the rest of the stained glass. Then Father Neves, the only person who had remained calm, went over to the door where the sacristan had fled and, unhurriedly, let the women and children into the sacristy. He called again and again for calm, but outside the shouts and threats got louder and louder and more stones came flying in. Crammed together in the sacristy, people were saying it was an uprising in the *musseques* and that they were trying to kill the soldiers who'd been provoking people all morning, banging on doors and windows and calling all the women and girls whores, spitting in the faces of the old people and invading their homes.

There were a lot of soldiers, going around in groups of three or four, provoking people and trying to stir things up. Even today nobody really knows how it started – without so much as a word passing between the *musseques*, people grabbed barrel hoops, machetes, sticks and stones and came into the streets to defend their women, to fight the soldiers and to die if need be.

When the trouble began, I grabbed Carmindinha and, along with Zeca Bunéu, we pushed the terrified Mrs Domingas into the sacristy. There was a door from the room out into a courtyard filled with plants and flowers, and an open window from where Zeca, Carmindinha and I saw something we'll never forget: a huge crowd of people, men and women, old and young, screaming and shouting, their faces full of anger, kids flinging stones at the windows and into the church, while others brandished their barrel hoops, machetes and knives. Father Neves took one look at them and, better than anyone, he could see in their eyes the fear, the centuries old fear, rising from the darkness inside and coursing through their thin, insulted bodies, shaking their weapons and calling for the soldiers to be handed over.

Father Neves went over to the window and tried to talk to them. Almost everyone there knew him, but only a great wall of voices answered him, and the good man turned back towards us, his eyes full of tears.

'Dear God! There's nothing I can do!'

That's exactly how we all felt. From far away, carried by the wind, came the sounds of even worse to come. A distant crackle and screech of cars accelerating, and only the noise of the crowd clamouring for the soldiers stopped us hearing clearly what was happening out of sight. Deep down we could already guess. Then, coming closer, there were shots, shouts, people running in all directions, hiding in the first open doorway or backyard they came to. The women in the sacristy stopped praying and fixed their eyes on the window from where these new sounds came, the sound of shots and the rumbling of jeeps and police vans piling through the *musseques,* trampling over the people and their homes.

Into the great silence that followed the shots came screams as people dropped everything and grabbed their children, soldiers and policemen yelling, clouds of dust as walls collapsed and, driving everything, the dry spluttering cough of sub-machine gun fire spraying back and forth across the houses. Bodies lay stretched out on the sandy ground, some staring motionless at the sky, others writhing in agony as the sand reddened with their blood.

Father Neves rushed over to pull Zeca away from the window and close it against the inferno outside. But Zeca wanted to see everything that was going on. So, God forgive him, Father Neves slapped Zeca a couple of times across the face and pulled him down onto the floor, then slammed the window shut. But still the noise came in through the gaps in the broken glass.

Even today, whenever Zeca tells the story his eyes widen with the same fear and anger as when Father Neves slapped his face and dragged him away from the window. Zeca looked over at me, kneeling beside Mrs Domingas and Carmindinha, praying to God and all the saints as commanded by our priest. And then, until the prayers drowned everything out, at least from our ears if not from our hearts, he just covered his eyes and ears like a child.

3

If I hadn't been there myself and had just heard it from someone else, I'd never have believed it even if they'd sworn on the blood of Christ and crossed themselves with their own spit, the way we used to do. And I'd never have believed it because I'd been taught – like all of us, some with a belt and some with a stick – that what your father tells you is always right and you're just a kid and you should never argue with your elders and betters.

And if, before it happened, my feelings for Carmindinha were only just beginning, then that was the moment I really knew I was in love. A girl of sixteen saying the things we all wanted to say, talking to grown-ups the way we didn't yet know how, or were too scared to. A girl, tall and slim, wearing a pretty chintz dress she'd made with her own nimble fingers, answering back to her father, Captain Bento de Jesus Abano, ship's master, man of the sea and of life itself, with over fifty years of trials and tribulations and whose word was law in the *musseque*. When Bento spoke, he spoke the truth, even if we didn't always want to believe it.

But everything changed that Sunday of the broken windows and the bloodstained sands. We knew it from the smugness in Mr Antunes's face when we ran down to the grocery store with our errands, or from Mrs Domingas's downcast eyes when she came out of the shop and Dona Branca and Dona Eva pretended not to see her, all those years of familiar greetings and borrowed cups of salt, sugar and flour, all forgotten. Or when Carmindinha came back from class – now she was the one teaching the other girls – complaining about all the insults and abuse she was getting, even in the city centre.

What made it even more difficult to believe was the absolute certainty and truth of the words she spoke, straight from the wisdom of her heart and the proof of her own eyes, those same eyes as Bento Abano's, that had seen the people clamouring for the soldiers, throwing sticks and stones and then fleeing, and then the little wisps of dust and sand from the spluttering rifles and machine guns.

The captain strode around the room, his voice raised. Carmindinha was sitting down, nervously working the needle and thread with her agile fingers. I kept my head down, trying to duck under the force of the words that flew about the room.

'Silence, girl! I won't tell you again. Obey your father!'

She carried on sewing, more quickly now.

'You're nothing but a child!' the captain continued scornfully. 'What do you know about life? Well? What do you know about people dying? It's what I've always said: the people just don't have any respect for themselves!'

Carmindinha jumped out of her chair, her eyes bulging from the effort to contain herself, but she couldn't hold back.

'Oh I know all right! Respect? What respect? They bang on your door, they insult your daughter, and you stand there with your respect, your precious good manners, and you don't let it get to you? Is that it? And then you say the only thing our people want these days is wine, women, stealing, wearing a fancy suit and tie or what have you, and that the men aren't what they used to be?'

The old captain turned, his eyes shining as he fought to get the words out.

'Respect and you'll be respected! How are they going to earn respect if they don't take any care of themselves? They don't study! They don't learn! They don't broaden their minds! Living like pagans, only interested in women, whoring around at the dance halls, messing around with witch doctors and all the rest of it. No concern at all for the mind. No one can insult a man with a mind – he's got his mind to fall back on!'

I listened, baffled by Bento Abano's words, and I remembered all the things he'd written in those old newspapers that he'd shown me and Zeca, and, at that moment, I just couldn't figure out who was right. The fabric turned and turned in Carmindinha's nervous hands, and Bento Abano lowered his gaze. Her face was bright red, the blood rushing just beneath her clear skin. She stood up, struggling to put in order the words racing around her head.

'Broaden their minds? How? What about the schools? And as for the wine and dance halls and drinking dens, why don't they just put a stop to it all? Well? Why don't they just close them all down?'

Bento Abano stood by the doorway and filled his lungs with the cool evening air.

He turned and smiled. The twinkle had returned to his eye and he delayed his reply, certain now that he was winning the argument. But Carmindinha was in full flow.

'Ah! So you don't know, then? That's what I mean – their excuse is just the same! "The people aren't up to it, they've been spoilt, this generation's only interested in drinking and whoring…" Don't you see?'

My jaw hung wide open. Zeca, crouching in a corner, watched the scene with his big, curious eyes, and you could see he didn't want the argument ever to end – a girl of sixteen, fighting with her old dad who knew everything there was to know – it was the kind of thing people would talk about in our *musseque* for a long time. Bento Abano changed tack, putting on a superior, mocking tone – we could tell he didn't like losing.

'Back in the old days, my girl... Look, I don't blame you for what you say – you're still a little girl and you don't think with your head, you just talk with your heart. Life will teach you soon enough...'

Carmindinha leapt up. 'You're calling *me* a little girl?' she screamed back at him. 'I'm the one bringing money into this house! I'm not a child, I'm a woman!'

But Bento was warming to his new tone and wasn't going to let go, even in the face of Carmindinha's anger.

'As I was saying, back in the old days, we could demand things. Justice even. The young people in this country took the trouble to learn things, they cultivated their minds, got themselves an education, made something of themselves. Their fellow citizens respected them, the people had their chiefs, and everyone knew who they were. There were no arguments. And now what?'

He wasn't talking to Carmindinha any more. He was saying these things only to himself, trying to forget, to flee, to remind himself that he was right.

'Yes, father. And now what? What happened to them? All that writing and talking – were they the only ones who knew anything? Everyone who came after them not worth a damn? All idiots? Morons?'

How could Carmindinha say things like that? Sometimes when the captain showed us his newspapers from the old days and talked about the people in his Angolan Literary Association with their flimsy handwritten magazine just like the one Zeca and I were starting now, yes, there were some things I couldn't make head nor tail of. How come I was only now beginning to understand what Carmindinha was talking about?

Captain Bento didn't reply. Instead, his eyes still glistening but his voice softening, he started coming out with random words, names of people, newspapers, rummaging around for some of his old press cuttings. He picked up one article and started to read aloud, 'Education: the Source of Enlightenment', his voice straining, almost shouting himself hoarse so that Zeca and I, still crouching in the corner, could hear him. Carmindinha, standing in the middle of the room, her sewing strewn on the floor and her face flushed red, was furious.

'That's all over now, dead and gone!' she screamed at her father, the last ounce of respect gone from her voice. 'Do you hear me, captain? It's over, finished, kaput! It's too late to sit here hoping that Zeca's going to cultivate his mind, that I'm going to cultivate my mind, that we're all going to cultivate our minds and set up our own little literary association! Come off it, dad! With all this 'respect' they're going to have for us,' she carried on, her voice turning even more sarcastic, 'do you really think the soldiers are going to stop banging on our doors to get us to sleep with them, or beating up the street vendors because they don't have change? It's over! Dead and buried, for Christ's sake!'

She went out and slammed the door behind her. A well-brought-up girl like her – none of us knew what to think. We looked around the room, at her sewing things lying abandoned on the floor, and couldn't think of anything to say. Bento managed a smile as if trying to show he'd won, but when we looked into his eyes, the captain's eyes we knew so well, we could see that deep down they had lost their shine, and those hands which had held the *Good Journey* so firmly on its course now trembled as he gripped the yellowing scraps of newspaper in their faded cardboard folder.

'Go now,' he told us. 'Go over to Don'Ana's and tell my family to come back here. I'm hungry.'

His voice was sad, old and hoarse, straining to still sound

like the voice we used to know, the voice that gave the orders. He looked at us with those eyes that once again were clouding over with the memories of life, and said,

'Don't you ever forget what you heard here, boy. Put it all in your newspaper so that everyone will know.'

And he showed us out into the street, into the cool night air.

4

The coffin was long and narrow, just like its owner. And it didn't have all those decorations – flowers, pretty little silver-coloured angels or whatever – that Zeca added when he wrote in the newspaper about our dear friend's death. It was narrow and black, with just a couple of silver lines running around it. Very sober, just as the deceased had wanted it, and nobody was going to disobey him. Even when he started to throw up those little flecks of black blood that the doctor said were his liver, Bento Abano carried on talking like he always had, carried on believing that nothing had changed. And no one could forget his calm, pensive words, day after day telling Mrs Domingas to forgive their daughter Tunica and telling Carmindinha how proud he was, asking her always to be a good girl, to study hard and to look after her mother who wasn't getting any younger. Then, when Zeca and I spoke of Xoxombo, he'd cry a soft, silent tear of pain and suffering that was greater than his illness. He was in bed for six months, feeling this creature gnawing away at his insides, waiting with his usual courage for death to come. Right to the end, he read our newspaper, always explaining, always correcting, always teaching. We watched his thin, sunburnt, worn-out body shrinking with each day that passed, his skin turning the colour of sand from the beach and pulling tightly at the bones of his face and arms, his skinny, obstinate fingers jabbing the air as he spoke, his words growing husky and getting lost in the hurried breath of his tired lungs.

So there he was inside that simple coffin lying on the table covered with black cloth, six candles to provide light for the people sitting on the floor, out in the yard, and in Mrs Domingas's bedroom. Only Zeca was there with him when he died, and the thick, hot, black blood covered the old man's hand as he clutched the boy, looking up at him with a still, serene smile, stained and discoloured by his wasted liver. Only his staring eyes betrayed his death. Empty, silent and lifeless – even the spider's web of wrinkles around his eyes seemed to melt away, as if death had quietly erased all the pain and happiness that they recorded. We found out later that Zeca's dad – sobbing loudly in a way no one in the *musseque* thought him capable of – quarrelled with the coffin man, insisting that he himself give the captain his last shave. Then he washed him and dressed him in his black suit that was now far too big for his shrivelled body; his face seemed almost to be apologising for being that way. But his smile, fixed on his face by death, was the last of many gifts our great friend gave us, and that will stay with us forever.

Sitting on the floor mats, some of Mrs Domingas's oldest friends filled the room with a steady, constant wail accompanied by a rocking of the head and a rhythmic, sobbing, tearless lament. They asked the departing soul to take messages to their dead kinsfolk, begged forgiveness for long-forgotten deeds and, since they were talking only in Kimbundu, said other things I couldn't understand.

In the bedroom, Carmindinha by her side, Mrs Domingas was saying how her grief was already spent after six months of waiting and that death had long since left her. In the backyard, underneath the *mulemba* tree, the boys and girls who'd come with their parents to mourn the death and console their relatives, played with Bebiana and Tété – they were already growing into little girls and wouldn't stay at home in bed when Don'Ana came to mourn with her friend. They played quietly and happily with their little pebbles, and I thought to myself that inside his coffin Captain Bento would be enjoying listening to their little voices, already missing bouncing Bebiana on his knee like he used to. She hadn't cried or looked at all shocked when they told her that the captain was going to live in heaven and would never be coming back. She just looked with those big, moist eyes of hers and said casually,

'Oh! Well, someday I'll go there too.'

Lightly and without a sound, Carmindinha passed through into her bedroom. I could feel Zeca's eyes glance over at me. He knew all about it – it had been many months since she and I had our big bust-up outside the high school and I still hadn't managed to patch things up. I tried to get Tereza and Joanica involved, and I waited for her outside the sewing school. She'd still turn up in the evenings to chat and stuff, but she hadn't forgiven me.

That night, with the old captain taking his last voyage in that narrow little ship of his, I felt like giving up. Carmindinha had grown up and was now an adult. I felt like a child. I needed to forget her. My thoughts returned to the old sailor, our friend. I looked over at the coffin. It was the first time I'd seen a dead body. I'd never imagined dying would be like this, simple and quiet and still. I'd thought people would shout and cry and try to escape. What do people die for? I thought of asking Zeca, but held my tongue. Mind you, living forever was no better. People meet, talk, work, their lives collide, they get married, have kids, and then they die. It hurt to think about it – there was nothing I could remember about life without death coming into it somehow. If I died I'd never see Zeca again, never finish our newspaper, never see my friends at school, our *musseque*, Carmindinha. I felt sorry about the things I wouldn't do any more, and sorry about the things I'd already planned to do when I was grown up. That was the worst of it all, not seeing, not talking, not being with people. So no, I didn't want to die.

Carmindinha walked back through the room again and the flames of the candles danced.

It was a dark, hot night. There was only a light breeze, giving the air a deceptive freshness that seemed to get even hotter as it drifted up towards the other huts, rustling almost inaudibly in the leaves of the trees. You could feel the heat like an invisible blanket covering our *musseque*, leaving a thick, heavy sweat sticking to your shirt and hands. Mixed with the smells of burning wax, flowers and food, it made me feel sick. I went and stood at the doorway.

I opened my arms to the darkness, looked up at the stars in the black cloth of the sky and once again Captain Bento was with me, navigating through the night. I walked slowly over to Don'Ana's house, whispering softly the names of the stars up above, the names the captain had taught us that night on the deck of the *Good Journey*, and I searched for my favourites. Far in the distance, right on the dark line where Earth merges into Heaven, was the big, bright, happy star Maneco Santo had pointed out that night. A lump came into my throat when I remembered that the star was Carmindinha.

A faint pool of light escaping from the door of the dead man's house pulled me out of my reverie. It was Carmindinha, leaning against the frame of the half-opened door. Her eyes shone in the darkness, but they were no longer the eyes of the girl I used to know. It's true she was older than me, sixteen already, but for me it was like we were still children messing around.

I walked up to her slowly and stopped in front of those eyes – the same eyes as the old sea captain's, only younger. Happiness stole the words from my mouth and tears I didn't even know I had ran down my face as I felt her hot, luminous skin lean against me. It was Carmindinha's soft voice – I'd only once in my life heard her angry, the time she'd had that argument with her dad after all the trouble with the soldiers at the Mission. I couldn't speak. I just let our love sleep softly between us – Carmindinha was there and nothing else mattered.

'There, there,' she murmured. 'Don't cry. Come on, don't cry…'

Tears, hot like the night, ran through my fingers. I walked slowly through the sand of our *musseque*, Carmindinha close beside me, her skirt creating the softest of breezes, and her feet sliding almost silently across the sand. Far off in the distance shone the Southern Cross.

'Do you see that big star? The bright one?'

She didn't answer. I pulled her thin, hot body closer. She turned towards me and her hair rustled faintly as she tilted her head to look up at the sky.

'It's you!'

Her small, neat breasts trembled in my hands as she let out a childish laugh. We were underneath the *muxixi* tree behind Don'Ana's house and I could feel the rough grass beneath our feet. A grassy, earthy smell swathed our bodies and washed over our clothes scattered on the ground. My hands searched hungrily, blindly, and a strong smell, a good smell that came from the heat of the night and all the smells of the houses and the grasses and the trees of our *musseque*, blossomed from

Carmindinha's little hands.

So that hot night while the old captain smiled his eternal smile, Carmindinha and I loved each other with our gleaming bodies, wrapped in the thick blanket of the deep, black, moonless, starry night, as our hands and eyes had for so long longed to do.

And when the cock crowed, calling us from our saddened happiness and reminding us what time it was, we walked back through the long grass, arm in arm, and rejoined the others, tired and silent at the old captain's vigil. Among them it was only Zeca who noticed in our eyes what everyone in our *musseque* had known for a long time: that Carmindinha and I were in love.

That's all.

*

The lifeless portrait still watches over us. Its grey background is already yellowing with age, but it's the same man – peaceful and good, although angry and harsh in his righteousness – that our *musseque* knew.

And it's those eyes, full of the life he saw and lived, that he bequeathed to Carmindinha, whose warm, moist body now lies beside me. The eyes I first saw slipping away from the defeated face of the old captain on the day of their big argument, only for them to be reborn that very same moment in his daughter, victorious but sad too as she watched her father retreat to his corner, shuffling the bits of old newspaper cuttings he'd produced as his final vindication, but which had failed to overcome the simple truth of Carmindinha's words and all the things she'd said about the blood, shame and tears that seeped through the sands of the *musseque*, hardening the tyre tracks of the trucks carrying away the prisoners.

It seemed then to me that ship's captain, Bento de Jesus Abano was from another time, just like that old yellow portrait on the wall. But that look of his hiding beneath the peak of his sailor's cap, those eyes caught in their spider's web of wrinkles – why were they still speaking to us? Why were they always telling us something new, or showing us something old that we had forgotten?

Zeca Bunéu used to say that without that look, there would be no Carmindinha.

São Paulo Prison, Luanda
December 1961 – April 1962

Translator's Note

Our Musseque is a book about telling stories. Sometimes the narrator carefully dissects different versions trying to work out the truth, sometimes he blithely tells us things he couldn't possibly have seen. Stories are told and retold, embroidered and simplified, in a continuation of an African and universal, storytelling tradition.

As we slip back and forwards in time, we're sometimes left wondering what actually happened, to whom and when, and yet we never really doubt that the book is absolutely true to what it describes. Luandino Vieira draws heavily on his own childhood experiences growing up in the *musseque*, and while the ending of the book (written in prison in 1961–62) clearly resonates with the 1959–61 chain of events that sparked the beginning of Angola's war of independence, it actually describes, tellingly, a much earlier uprising in 1944. Father Neves was indeed the parish priest in 1944 and, as Canon Manuel das Neves, he played an active role later on in the independence struggle, with which Luandino Vieira was of course himself closely involved. The book's temporal fluidity in itself tells us much.

Just as the narrator and the author are retelling stories they have heard, so this translation is a retelling – a faithful one, I hope. Luandino Vieira wrote the novel in a unique and in its time controversial style, representing the language spoken in the shanty towns of Luanda – partly Portuguese and partly Kimbundu, from which he formed his own, closely observed, synthesis. I concluded, somewhat reluctantly, that it would be folly to attempt to recreate this particular linguistic blend in English, and so my approach has been to tell the stories in the language that I hear the characters speak and which I think they themselves heard, without the linguistic variations that are such an essential feature of the Portuguese text.

I am indebted to Anthony Soares for introducing me to *Nosso Musseque*, to Dedalus Books and English PEN for making this translation possible, to Margaret Jull Costa for her steadfast encouragement and invaluable advice, to Pedro Gonçalves da Silva for his patience and understanding, and to Luandino Vieira for his generous and illuminating responses to my questions. Any mistakes and errors of judgment in this translation remain, of course, my own.

Robin Patterson
Lisbon, August 2014